FLAT STANLEY
Collection

FLAT STANLEY

Collection

by Jeff Brown
Illustrated by Jon Mitchell

EGMONT

EGMONT

We bring stories to life

First published in Great Britain 2013 by Egmont UK Limited
The Yellow Building, 1 Nicholas Road, London W11 4AN

Text copyright © 1985 Jeff Brown
Illustrations copyright © 2012 by the Trust
u/w/o Richard C. Brown a/k/a/Jeff Brown
f/b/o Duncan Brown

ISBN 978 1 4052 6658 1

www.egmont.co.uk

A CIP catalogue record for this title is available from the British Library

Printed and bound in Great Britain by the CPI Group

44266/9

FLAT STANLEY

The Big Bulletin Board

Breakfast was ready.

'I will go and wake the boys,' Mrs Lambchop said to her husband, George Lambchop. Just then their younger son, Arthur, called from the bedroom he shared with his brother Stanley.

'Hey! Come and look! Hey!'

Mr and Mrs Lambchop were both very much in favour of politeness and careful speech. 'Hay is for horses, Arthur, not people,' Mr Lambchop said as they entered the bedroom. 'Try to remember that.'

'Excuse me,' Arthur said. 'But look!'

He pointed to Stanley's bed. Across it lay the enormous bulletin board that Mr Lambchop had given the boys a Christmas ago, so that they could pin up pictures and messages and maps. It had fallen, during the night, on top of Stanley.

But Stanley was not hurt. In fact he would still have been sleeping if he had not been woken by his brother's shout.

'What's going on here?' he called out cheerfully from beneath the enormous board.

Mr and Mrs Lambchop hurried to lift it from the bed.

'Heavens!' said Mrs Lambchop.

'Gosh!' said Arthur. 'Stanley's flat!'

'As a pancake,' said Mr Lambchop. 'Darndest thing I've ever seen.'

'Let's all have breakfast,' Mrs Lambchop said. 'Then Stanley and I will go and see Doctor Dan and hear what he has to say.'

The examination was almost over.

'How do you feel?' Doctor Dan asked. 'Does it hurt very much?'

'I felt sort of tickly for a while after I got up,' Stanley Lambchop said, 'but I feel fine now.'

'Well, that's mostly how it is with these cases,' said Doctor Dan.

'We'll just have to keep an eye on this young fellow,' he said when he had finished the examination. 'Sometimes we doctors, despite all our years of training and experience, can only marvel at how little we really know.'

Mrs Lambchop said she thought that Stanley's clothes would have to be altered by the tailor now, so Doctor Dan told his nurse to take Stanley's measurements.

Mrs Lambchop wrote them down.

Stanley was four feet tall, about a foot wide, and half an inch thick.

Chapter Two

Being Flat

When Stanley got used to being flat, he enjoyed it.

He could go in and out of rooms, even when the door was closed, just by lying down and sliding through the crack at the bottom.

Mr and Mrs Lambchop said it was silly, but they were quite proud of him.

Arthur got jealous and tried to slide under

a door, but he just banged his head.

Being flat could also be helpful, Stanley found.

He was taking a walk with Mrs Lambchop one afternoon when her favourite ring fell from her finger. The ring rolled across the pavement and down between the bars of a grating that covered a dark, deep shaft.

Mrs Lambchop began to cry.

'I have an idea,' Stanley said.

He took the laces out of his shoes and an extra pair out of his pocket and tied them all together to make one long lace. Then he tied the end of that to the back of his belt and gave the other end to his mother.

'Lower me,' he said, 'and I will look for the ring.'

'Thank you, Stanley,' Mrs Lambchop said. She lowered him between the bars and moved him carefully up and down and from side to side, so that he could search the whole floor of the shaft.

Two policemen came by and stared at Mrs Lambchop as she stood holding the long lace that ran down through the grating. She pretended not to notice them.

'What's the matter, lady?' the first policeman asked. 'Is your yo-yo stuck?'

'I am not playing with a yo-yo!' Mrs Lambchop said sharply. 'My son is at the other end of this lace, if you must know.'

'Get the net, Harry,' said the second policeman. 'We have caught a cuckoo!'

Just then, down in the shaft, Stanley cried out, 'Hooray!'

Mrs Lambchop pulled him up and saw that he had the ring.

'Good for you, Stanley,' she said. Then she turned angrily to the policemen.

'A cuckoo, indeed!' she said. 'Shame!'

The policemen apologised. 'We didn't get it, lady,' they said. 'We have been hasty. We see that now.'

'People should think twice before making

rude remarks,' said Mrs Lambchop. 'And
then not make them at all.'

The policemen realised that was a good
rule and said they would try to remember it.

One day Stanley got a letter from his friend
Thomas Anthony Jeffrey, whose family had

moved recently to California. A school holiday was about to begin and Stanley was invited to spend it with the Jeffreys.

'Oh, boy!' Stanley said. 'I would love to go!'

Mr Lambchop sighed. 'A round trip train or aeroplane ticket to California is very expensive,' he said. 'I shall have to think of some cheaper way.'

When Mr Lambchop came home from the office that evening, he brought with him an enormous brown-paper envelope.

'Now then, Stanley,' he said. 'Try this for size.'

The envelope fitted Stanley very well. There was even room left over, Mrs Lambchop discovered, for an egg-salad sandwich made with thin bread, and a flat cigarette case filled with milk.

They had to put a great many stamps on the envelope to pay for both airmail and insurance, but it was still much less expensive than a train or aeroplane ticket to California would have been.

The next day Mr and Mrs Lambchop slid Stanley into his envelope, along with the egg-salad sandwich and the cigarette case full of milk, and mailed him from the box on the corner. The envelope had to be folded to fit through the slot, but Stanley was a limber boy and inside the box he straightened up again.

Mrs Lambchop was nervous because Stanley had never been away from home alone before. She rapped on the box.

'Can you hear me, dear?' she called. 'Are you all right?'

Stanley's voice came quite clearly. 'I'm fine. Can I eat my sandwich now?'

'Wait an hour. And try not to get overheated, dear,' Mrs Lambchop said. Then she and Mr Lambchop cried out 'Good-bye, good-bye!' and went home.

Stanley had a fine time in California. When the visit was over, the Jeffreys returned him in a beautiful white envelope they had made themselves. It had red-and-blue markings to show that it was airmail, and Thomas Jeffrey had lettered it 'Valuable' and 'Fragile' and 'This End Up' on both sides.

Back home Stanley told his family that he had been handled so carefully he never felt a single bump. Mr Lambchop said it proved that jet planes were wonderful, and so was

the Post Office Department, and that this
was a great age in which to live.

Stanley thought so too.

Chapter Three

Stanley the Kite

Mr Lambchop had always liked to take the boys off with him on Sunday afternoons to a museum or roller-skating in the park, but it was difficult when they were crossing streets or moving about in crowds. Stanley and Arthur would often be jostled from his side and Mr Lambchop worried about speeding taxis or that hurrying people might accidentally knock them down.

It was easier after Stanley got flat.

Mr Lambchop discovered that he could roll Stanley up without hurting him at all. He would tie a piece of string around Stanley to keep him from unrolling and make a little loop in the string for himself. It was as simple as carrying a parcel, and he could hold on to Arthur with the other hand.

Stanley did not mind being carried because he had never much liked to walk. Arthur didn't like walking either, but he had to. It made him mad.

One Sunday afternoon, in the street, they met an old college friend of Mr Lambchop's, a man he had not seen for years.

'Well, George, I see you have bought some wallpaper,' the man said. 'Going to decorate your house, I suppose?'

'Wallpaper?' said Mr Lambchop. 'Oh, no. This is my son Stanley.'

He undid the string and Stanley unrolled.

'How do you do?' Stanley said.

'Nice to meet you, young feller,' the man said. He said to Mr Lambchop, 'George, that boy is flat.'

'Smart, too,' Mr Lambchop said. 'Stanley is third from the top in his class at school.'

'Phooey!' said Arthur.

'This is my younger son, Arthur,' Mr Lambchop said. 'And he will apologise for his rudeness.'

Arthur could only blush and apologise.

Mr Lambchop rolled Stanley up again and they set out for home. It rained quite hard while they were on the way. Stanley, of course, hardly got wet at all, just around the edges, but Arthur got soaked.

Late that night Mr and Mrs Lambchop heard a noise out in the living room. They found Arthur lying on the floor near the bookcase. He had piled a great many volumes of the *Encyclopaedia Britannica* on top of himself.

'Put some more on me,' Arthur said when he saw them. 'Don't just stand there. Help me.'

Mr and Mrs Lambchop sent him back to bed, but the next morning they spoke to Stanley. 'Arthur can't help being jealous,' they said. 'Be nice to him. You're his big brother, after all.'

Stanley and Arthur were in the park. The day was sunny, but windy too, and many older boys were flying beautiful, enormous kites with long tails, made in all the colours of the rainbow.

Arthur sighed. 'Some day,' he said, 'I will have a big kite and I will win a kite-flying contest and be famous like everyone else. *Nobody* knows who I am these days.'

Stanley remembered
what his parents had
said. He went to a
boy whose kite was
broken and borrowed
a large spool of string.

'You can fly me, Arthur,'
he said. 'Come on.'

He attached the string to
himself and gave Arthur the
spool to hold. He ran lightly
across the grass, sideways
to get up speed, and then
he turned to meet the
breeze.

Up, up, up . . . UP!
went Stanley, being
a kite.

He knew just how to manage on the gusts of wind. He faced full into the wind if he wanted to rise, and let it take him from behind when he wanted speed. He had only to turn his thin edge to the wind, carefully, a little at a time, so that it did not hold him, and then he would slip gracefully down towards the earth again.

Arthur let out all the string and Stanley soared high above the trees, a beautiful sight in his pale sweater and bright brown trousers, against the pale-blue sky.

Everyone in the park stood still to watch.

Stanley swooped right and then left in long, matched swoops. He held his arms by his sides and zoomed at the ground like a rocket and curved up again towards the sun. He sideslipped and circled, and made figure

eights and crosses and a star.

Nobody has ever flown the way Stanley Lambchop flew that day. Probably no one ever will again.

After a while, of course, people grew tired of watching and Arthur got tired of running about with the empty spool. Stanley went right on though, showing off.

Three boys came up to Arthur and invited him to join them for a hot dog and some soda pop. Arthur left the spool wedged in the fork of a tree. He did not notice, while he was eating the hot dog, that the wind was blowing the string and tangling it about the tree.

The string got shorter and shorter, but Stanley did not realise how low he was until

leaves brushed his feet, and then it was too late. He got stuck in the branches. Fifteen minutes passed before Arthur and the other boys heard his cries and climbed up to set him free.

Stanley would not speak to his brother that evening, and at bedtime, even though Arthur had apologised, he was still cross.

Alone with Mr Lambchop in the living room, Mrs Lambchop sighed and shook her head. 'You're at the office all day, having fun,' she said. 'You don't realise what I go through with the boys. They're very difficult.'

'Kids are like that,' Mr Lambchop said. 'Phases. Be patient, dear.'

The Museum Thieves

Mr and Mrs O. J. Dart lived in the flat just above the Lambchops. Mr Dart was an important man, the director of a Famous Museum of Art in the city.

Stanley Lambchop had noticed in the lift that Mr Dart, who was ordinarily a cheerful man, had become quite gloomy, but he had no idea what the reason was. And then at breakfast one morning he heard Mr and

Mrs Lambchop talking about Mr Dart.

'I see,' said Mr Lambchop, reading the paper over his coffee cup, 'that still another painting has been stolen from the Famous Museum. It says here that Mr O.J. Dart, the director, is at his wits' end.'

MUSEUM ART
STOLEN AGAIN!

'Oh, dear! Are the police no help?' Mrs Lambchop asked.

'It seems not,' said Mr Lambchop. 'Listen to what the Chief of Police told the newspaper. "We suspect a gang of sneak thieves. These are the worst kind. They work by sneakery, which makes them very difficult to catch. However, my men and I will keep trying. Meanwhile, I hope people will buy tickets for the Policemen's Ball and not park their cars where signs say don't."'

The next morning Stanley Lambchop heard Mr Dart talking to his wife in the lift.

'These sneak thieves work at night,' Mr Dart said. 'It is very hard for our guards to stay awake when they have been on duty all day. And the Famous Museum

is so big we cannot guard every picture at the same time. I fear it is hopeless, hopeless, hopeless!'

Suddenly, as if an electric light bulb had lit up in the air above his head, giving out little shooting lines of excitement, Stanley Lambchop had an idea. He told it to Mr Dart.

'Stanley,' Mr Dart said, 'if your mother will give her permission, I will put you and your plan to work this very night!'

Mrs Lambchop gave her permission. 'But you will have to take a long nap this afternoon,' she said. 'I won't have you up till all hours unless you do.'

That evening, after a long nap, Stanley went with Mr Dart to the Famous Museum. Mr Dart took him into the main hall, where

the biggest and most important paintings were hung. He pointed to a huge painting that showed a bearded man, wearing a floppy velvet hat, playing a violin for a lady who lay on a couch. There was a half-man, half-horse person standing behind them, and three fat children with wings were flying around above. That, Mr Dart explained, was

the most expensive painting in the world!

There was an empty picture frame on the opposite wall. We shall hear more about that later on.

Mr Dart took Stanley into his office and said, 'It is time for you to put on a disguise.'

'I had already thought of that,' Stanley Lambchop said, 'and I brought one. My

cowboy suit. It has a red bandanna that I can tie over my face. Nobody will recognise me in a million years.'

'No,' Mr Dart said. 'You will have to wear the disguise I have chosen.'

From a closet he took a white dress with a blue sash, a pair of shiny little pointed shoes, a wide straw hat with a blue band that matched the sash, and a wig and a stick.

The wig was made of blonde hair, long and done in ringlets. The stick was curved at the top and it, too, had a blue ribbon on it.

'In this shepherdess disguise,' Mr Dart said, 'you will look like a painting that belongs in the main hall. We do not have cowboy pictures in the main hall.'

Stanley was so disgusted that he could

hardly speak. 'I shall look like a girl, that's what I shall look like,' he said. 'I wish I had never had my idea.'

But he was a good sport, so he put on the disguise.

Back in the main hall Mr Dart helped Stanley climb up into the empty picture frame. Stanley was able to stay in place because Mr Dart had cleverly put four small spikes in the wall, one for each hand and foot.

The frame was a perfect fit. Against the wall, Stanley looked just like a picture.

'Except for one thing,' Mr Dart said. 'Shepherdesses are supposed to look happy. They smile at their sheep and at the sky. You look fierce, not happy, Stanley.'

Stanley tried hard to get a faraway look in

his eyes and even to smile a little bit.

Mr Dart stood back a few feet and stared at him for a moment. 'Well,' he said, 'it may not be art, but I know what I like.'

He went off to make sure that certain other parts of Stanley's plan were being taken care of, and Stanley was left alone.

It was very dark in the main hall. A little bit of moonlight came through the windows, and Stanley could just make out the world's most expensive painting on the opposite wall. He felt as though the bearded man with the violin and the lady on the couch and the half-horse person and the winged children were all waiting, as he was, for something to happen.

Time passed and he got tireder and tireder. Anyone would be tired this late at night, especially if he had to stand in a picture frame balancing on little spikes.

Maybe they won't come, Stanley thought. Maybe the sneak thieves won't come at all.

The moon went behind a cloud and then the main hall was pitch dark. It seemed to get quieter, too, with the darkness. There was absolutely no sound at all. Stanley felt the hair on the back of his neck prickle beneath the golden curls of the wig.

Cr-eee-eee-k . . .

The creaking sound came from right out in the middle of the main hall and even as he heard it Stanley saw, in the same place, a tiny yellow glow of light!

The creaking came again and the glow got bigger. A trap door had opened in the floor and two men came up through it into the hall!

Stanley understood everything all at once. These must be the sneak thieves! They had a secret trap door entrance into the museum from outside. That was why they had never been caught. And now, tonight,

they were back to steal the most expensive painting in the world!

He kept very still in his picture frame and listened to the sneak thieves.

'This is it, Max,' said the first one. 'This is where we art robbers pull a sensational job whilst the civilised community sleeps.'

'Right, Luther,' said the other man. 'In all this great city there is no one to suspect us.'

Ha, ha! thought Stanley Lambchop. That's what you think!

The sneak thieves put down their lantern and took the world's most expensive painting off the wall.

'What would we do to anyone who tried to capture us, Max?' the first man asked.

'We would kill him. What else?' his friend replied.

That was enough to frighten Stanley, and he was even more frightened when Luther came over and stared at him.

'This sheep girl,' Luther said. 'I thought sheep girls were supposed to smile, Max. This one looks scared.'

Just in time, Stanley managed to get a faraway look in his eyes again and to smile, sort of.

'You're crazy, Luther,' Max said. 'She's smiling. And what a pretty little thing she is, too.'

That made Stanley furious. He waited until the sneak thieves had turned back to the world's most expensive painting, and then he shouted in his loudest, most terrifying voice: 'POLICE! POLICE! MR DART! THE SNEAK THIEVES ARE HERE!'

The sneak thieves looked at each other. 'Max,' said the first one, very quietly, 'I think I heard the sheep girl yell.'

'I think I did too,' said Max in a quivery voice. 'Oh, boy! Yelling pictures. We both need a rest.'

'You'll get a rest, all right!' shouted Mr Dart, rushing in with the Chief of Police

and lots of guards and policemen behind him. 'You'll get *arrested*, that's what! Ha, ha, ha!'

The sneak thieves were too mixed up by Mr Dart's joke and too frightened by the policemen to put up a fight. Before they knew it, they had been handcuffed and led away to jail.

The next morning in the office of the Chief of Police Stanley Lambchop got a medal. The day after that his picture was in all the newspapers.

Chapter Five

Arthur's Good Idea

For a while Stanley Lambchop was a famous name. Everywhere that Stanley went, people stared and pointed at him. He could hear them whisper, 'Over there, Harriet, over there! That must be Stanley Lambchop, the one who caught the sneak thieves . . .' and things like that.

But after a few weeks the whispering and the staring stopped. People had other things to think about. Stanley did not mind. Being famous had been fun, but enough was enough.

And then came a further change, and it was not a pleasant one. People began to laugh and make fun of him as he passed by. 'Hello, Super-Skinny!' they would shout, and even ruder things, about the way he looked.

Stanley told his parents how he felt. 'It's the other kids I mostly mind,' he said. 'They don't like me any more because I'm different. Flat.'

'Shame on them,' Mrs Lambchop said. 'It is wrong to dislike people for their shapes. Or their religion, for that matter, or the colour of their skin.'

'I know,' Stanley said. 'Only maybe it's

impossible for everybody to like *everybody*.'

'Perhaps,' said Mrs Lambchop. 'But they can try.'

Later that night Arthur Lambchop was woken by the sound of crying. In the darkness he crept across the room and knelt by Stanley's bed.

'Are you okay?' he said.

'Go away,' Stanley said.

'Don't be mad at me,' Arthur said. 'You're still mad because I let you get tangled the day you were my kite, I guess.'

'Skip it, will you?' Stanley said. 'I'm not mad. Go away.'

'Please let's be friends . . .' Arthur couldn't help crying a little, too. 'Oh, Stanley,' he said. 'Please tell me what's wrong?'

Stanley waited for a long time before he

spoke. 'The thing is,' he said, 'I'm just not happy any more. I'm tired of being flat. I want to be a proper shape again, like other people. But I'll have to go on being flat for ever. It makes me sick.'

'Oh, Stanley,' Arthur said. He dried his tears on a corner of Stanley's sheet and could think of nothing more to say.

'Don't talk about what I just said,' Stanley told him. 'I don't want the folks to worry. That would only make it worse.'

'You're brave,' Arthur said. 'You really are.'

He took hold of Stanley's hand. The two brothers sat together in the darkness, being friends. They were both still sad, but each one felt a *little* better than he had before.

And then, suddenly, though he was not even trying to think, Arthur had an idea.

He jumped up and turned on the light and ran to the big storage box where toys and things were kept. He began to rummage in the box.

Stanley sat up in bed to watch.

Arthur flung aside a football and some lead soldiers and aeroplane models and lots of wooden blocks, and then he said, 'Aha!' He had found what he wanted – an old bicycle pump. He held it up, and Stanley and he looked at each other.

'Okay,' Stanley said at last. 'But take it easy.' He put the end of the long pump hose in his mouth and clamped his lips tightly about it so that no air could escape.

'I'll go slowly,' Arthur said. 'If it hurts or anything, wiggle your hand at me.'

He began to pump. At first nothing

happened except that Stanley's cheeks bulged a bit. Arthur watched his hand, but there was no wiggle signal, so he pumped on. Then, suddenly, Stanley's top half began to swell.

'It's working! It's working!' shouted Arthur, pumping away.

Stanley spread his arms so that the air could get round inside him more easily. He got bigger and bigger. The buttons of his pyjama top burst off – *Pop! Pop! Pop!* A moment more and he was all rounded out: head and body, arms and legs. But not his right foot. That foot stayed flat.

Arthur stopped pumping. 'It's like trying to do the very last bit of those long balloons,' he said. 'Maybe a shake would help.'

Stanley shook his right foot twice, and

with a little *whooshing* sound it swelled out
to match the left one. There stood Stanley
Lambchop as he used to be, as if he had
never been flat at all!

'Thank you, Arthur,' Stanley said. 'Thank
you very much.'

The brothers were shaking hands when
Mr Lambchop strode into the room with

Mrs Lambchop right behind him. 'We heard you!' said Mr Lambchop. 'Up and talking when you ought to be asleep, eh? Shame on –'

'GEORGE!' said Mrs Lambchop. 'Stanley's *round* again!'

'You're right!' said Mr Lambchop, noticing. 'Good for you, Stanley!'

'I'm the one who did it,' Arthur said. 'I blew him up.'

Everyone was terribly excited and happy, of course. Mrs Lambchop made hot chocolate to celebrate the occasion, and several toasts were drunk to Arthur for his cleverness.

When the little party was over, Mr and Mrs Lambchop tucked the boys back into their beds and kissed them, and then they

turned out the light. 'Goodnight,' they said.

'Goodnight,' said Stanley and Arthur.

It had been a long and tiring day. Very soon all the Lambchops were asleep.

FLAT STANLEY

Stanley and the Magic Lamp

Prologue

Once upon a very long time ago, way before the beginning of today's sort of people, there was a magical kingdom in which everyone lived forever, and anyone of importance was a genie, mostly the friendly kind. The few wicked genies kept out of sight in mountain caves or at the bottoms of rivers. They had no wish to provoke the great Genie King, who ruled very comfortably from an enormous palace with many towers and courtyards, and gardens with reflecting pools.

The Genie King took a special interest in the genie princes of the kingdom, and was noted for his patience with their high spirits and desire for adventure. The Genie Queen, in fact, thought he was *too* patient with them, and she said so one morning in the throne room, where the King was studying reports and proposals for new magic spells.

'Training, that's what they need. Discipline!' She adjusted the Magic Mirror on the throne-room wall. 'Florts and collibots! Granting wishes, which is what they'll be doing one day, is serious work.'

'Florts yourself! You're too hard on these lads,' said the Genie King, and then he frowned. 'This report here, though, says that one of them has been behaving very badly indeed.'

'Haraz, right?' said the Queen. 'He's the worst. What a smarty!'

The Genie King sent a thought to summon Prince Haraz, which is all such a ruler has to do when he wants somebody, and a moment later the young genie flew into the throne room, did a triple flip, and hovered in the air before the throne.

'That's no way to present yourself!' The Queen was furious. 'Really!'

Prince Haraz grinned. 'What's up?'

'You are!' said the King. 'Come down here!'

'No problem,' said the Prince, landing.

'It seems you have been playing a great many magical jokes,' said the King, tapping the reports before him. 'Very *annoying* jokes, such as causing the army's carpets to fly only in circles, which made all my soldiers dizzy.'

'That was a good one!' laughed the Prince.

'And turning the Chief Wizard's wand into a sausage while he was casting a major spell, you did that?'

'Ha, ha! You should have seen his face!' said the Prince.

'Stop laughing!' cried the Queen. 'Oh, this is shameful! You should be heavily punished!'

'He's just a boy, dear, only two hundred

years old,' said the King. 'But I'll –'

'Who knows what *more* he's done?' said the Queen, turning to the Magic Mirror. 'Magic Mirror, what other silly jokes has this fellow played!'

The Magic Mirror squirted apple juice all over her face and the front of her dress.

'Oooooohh!' The Queen whirled around. 'Florts and collibots! I know who's responsible for *that*!'

Prince Haraz blushed and tried to look sorry, but it was too late.

'That does it!' said the Genie King. 'Lamp duty for you, you rascal! One thousand years of service to a lamp.' He turned to the Queen. 'How's that, my dear?'

'Make it two thousand,' said the Queen, drying her face.

Prince Haraz

Almost a year had passed since Stanley Lambchop got over being flat, which he had become when his big bulletin board settled on him during the night. It had been a pleasant, restful time for all the Lambchops, as this particular evening was.

Dinner was over. In the living room, Mr Lambchop was reading and Mrs Lambchop was mending socks.

'How nice this is, my dear,' Mr Lambchop said. 'I am enjoying my newspaper, and your company, and the thought of our boys studying in their room.'

'Let us hope they *are* studying, George,' said Mrs Lambchop. 'So often they find excuses not to work.'

Mr Lambchop chuckled. 'They are very imaginative,' he said. 'No doubt of that.'

In their bedroom, Stanley and his younger brother, Arthur, had in fact begun their homework. They wore pyjamas, and over his Arthur also wore his Mighty Man T-shirt, which helped him to concentrate.

On the desk between them was what they supposed to be a teapot – a round, rather squashed-down pot with a curving spout, and a knob on top for lifting. A wave had rolled it up onto the beach that summer, right to Stanley's feet, and since Mrs Lambchop was very fond of old furniture and silverware, he had saved it as a gift for her birthday, now only a week away.

The pot was painted dark green, but streaks of brownish metal showed through where the green had rubbed off. To see if polishing would make it shine, Stanley rubbed the knob with his pyjama sleeve.

Puff! Black smoke came from the spout.

'Yipes!' Arthur said. 'It's going to explode!'

'Teapots don't explode.' Stanley rubbed again. 'I just –'

Puff! Puff! Puff! They came rapidly now, joining to form a small cloud in the air above the desk.

'Look out!' Arthur shouted. 'Double yipes!'

The black cloud swirled within itself, and its blackness became a mixture of brown and blue. A moment more, and it began to lose its cloud shape; arms appeared, and legs, and a head.

'Ready or not, here I come!' said a clear young voice.

And then the cloud was completely gone, and a slender, cheerful-looking body hovered in the air above the desk. He wore a sort of decorated towel on his head, a loose blue shirt, and curious, flapping brown trousers, one leg of which had snagged on the pot's spout.

'Florts!' said the boy, shaking his leg. 'Collibots! I got the puffs right, and the scary cloud, but – There!' Unsnagged, he floated down to the floor and bowed to Stanley and Arthur.

'Who rubbed?' he asked

Neither of the brothers could speak.

'Well, *someone* did. Genies don't just drop in, you know.' The boy bowed again. 'How do you do? I am Prince Fawzi Mustafa Aslan Mirza Melek Namerd Haraz. Call me Prince Haraz.'

Arthur gasped and dived under his bed.

'What's the matter with him?' the genie asked. 'And who are you, and where am I?'

'I'm Stanley Lambchop, and this is the United States of America,' Stanley said. 'That's my brother Arthur under the bed.'

'Not a very friendly welcome,' said Prince Haraz. 'Especially for someone who's been cooped up in a lamp.' Frowning, he rubbed the back of his neck. 'Florts! One thousand years, with my knees right up against my chin. This is my first time out.'

'I must have gone crazy,' said Arthur from under the bed. 'I am just going to lie here until a doctor comes.'

'Actually, Prince Haraz, you're here sort of by accident,' Stanley said. 'I didn't even know that pot was a lamp. Was it the rubbing? Those puffs of smoke, I mean, that turned into you?'

'Were you scared?' The genie laughed. 'Just a few puffs, I thought, and then I'll *whoooosh* up the spout!'

'Scaring *me* wasn't fair,' said Arthur, staying under the bed. 'I just live in this room because Stanley's my brother. It's his lamp, and he's the one who rubbed it.'

'Then he's the one I grant wishes for,' said Prince Haraz. 'Too bad for you.'

'I don't care,' said Arthur, but he did.

'Can I wish for anything?' Stanley asked. 'Anything at all?'

'Not if it's cruel or evil, or really nasty,' said Prince Haraz. 'I'm a lamp genie, you see, and we're the good kind. Not like those big jar genies. They're stinkers! Take my advice and stay away from big jars and urns – and if you do see one, don't rub it.'

'Wish for something, Stanley,' said Arthur, sounding suspicious. 'Test him out.'

'Wait,' Stanley said. 'I'll be right back.'

He went out into the living room, where Mr and Mrs Lambchop were still sitting quietly enjoying themselves.

'Hey!' he said. 'Guess what?'

'Hay is for horses, Stanley, not people,' said Mr Lambchop from behind his newspaper. 'Try to remember that.'

'Excuse me,' Stanley said. 'But you'll never guess –'

'My guess is that you and Arthur have not yet finished your homework,' said Mrs Lambchop, looking up from her mending. 'In fact, you can hardly have begun.'

'We *were* going to do it,' said Stanley, talking very fast, 'but I have this pot that turned out to be a lamp, and when I rubbed it smoke came out and then a genie, and he says I can wish for things, only I thought maybe I should ask you first. Arthur got scared, so he's hiding under the bed.'

Mr Lambchop chuckled. 'When your studying is done, my boy,' he said. 'But no treasure chests full of gold and diamonds, please. Think of the taxes we would pay!'

'There is your answer, Stanley,' said Mrs Lambchop. 'Now back to work, please.'

'Okay, then,' said Stanley, going out.

Mrs Lambchop laughed. 'Chests full of gold and diamonds, indeed. Taxes! George, you are very amusing.'

Behind his newspaper, Mr Lambchop smiled again. 'Thank you, my dear,' he said.

Chapter Two

The Askit Basket

'I told them, but they didn't believe me,' Stanley said, back in the bedroom.

'Of course they didn't.' Arthur was still under the bed. 'Who'd believe that a whole person could puff out of a pot?'

'It's not a *pot*,' said Prince Haraz. 'And this is a ridiculous way to carry on a conversation. Please come out. I apologise for the puffs.'

Arthur crawled from under the bed. 'No more scary stuff?'

'I promise,' the genie said, and they shook hands.

Arthur could hardly wait now. 'Try it Stanley,' he said. 'Try a wish.'

'We're not allowed,' Stanley said. 'Not till our homework is done.'

'What's homework?' Prince Haraz asked.

The brothers stared at him, amazed, and then Stanley explained. The genie shook his head.

'*After* schooltime, when you could be having fun?' he said. 'Where I come from, we just let Askit Baskets do the work.'

'Well, whatever *they* are, I wish I had one,' said Stanley, forgetting he was not supposed to wish.

Prince Haraz laughed. 'Oh? Look behind you.'

Turning, Stanley and Arthur saw a large straw basket, about the size of a beach ball and decorated with green and red zigzag stripes, floating in the air above the desk.

'Yipes!' said Arthur. 'More scary stuff!'

'Don't be silly,' said the genie. 'It's a perfectly ordinary Askit Basket. Whatever you want to know, Stanley, just ask it.'

Feeling rather foolish, Stanley leaned forward and spoke to the basket.

'I, uh . . . that is . . . uh,' he said. 'I'd like, uh . . . can I have answers for my maths homework? It's the problems on page twenty of my book.'

The basket made a steady *huuuummm* sound, and then the hum stopped and a

man's voice rose from it, deep and rich like a TV announcer's.

'Thank you for calling Askit Basket,' it said. 'Unfortunately, all our Answer Genies are busy at the present time, but your questions have been received, and you will be served by the first available personnel. While you wait, enjoy a selection by The Geniettes. This message will not be repeated.'

Stanley stared at the Askit Basket. Music was coming out of it now, the sort of soft,

faraway music he had heard in the elevators of big office buildings.

Prince Haraz shrugged. 'What can you do? It's a very popular service.'

There was a *click* and the music stopped. Now a female voice, full of bouncy good cheer, came from the basket. 'Hi! This is Shireen. Thanks a whole bunch for waiting, and I would like at this time to give you your answers. The first answer is: 5 pears, 6 apples, 8 bananas. The second answer is:

Tom is 4 years old, Tim is 7, Ted is 11. The third –'

'Let me get a pencil!' Stanley shouted. 'I can't remember all this!'

'A written record, created especially for your own personal convenience, is in the basket, sir,' said the cheery voice. 'Thanks for calling Askit Basket, and have a nice day!'

'Wait!' Lifting the lid of the basket, Stanley saw a sheet of paper with all his answers on it. 'Oh, good!' he said. 'Thank you. Can my brother talk now, please?'

Arthur cleared his throat. 'Hello Shireen,' he said. 'This is Arthur Lambchop speaking. For English, I'm supposed to write about "What I Want to Be". Could I have it printed out, please, like Stanley's maths?'

The answer came right away. 'Certainly, Mr Lambchop. Just a teeny-tiny moment now, while we make sure the handwriting – There! All done, Mr Lambchop!'

Arthur opened the basket and found a sheet of lined paper covered with his own handwriting. He read it aloud.

WHAT I WANT TO BE
by Arthur Lambchop

When I grow up I want to be President of the United States so that I can make a law not to have any more wars. And get to meet astronauts. And I would like to be handsome, only not have to go out with girls who want to get all dressed up. Most of all I would like to be the strongest man in the world, like Mighty Man, not to hurt people, but so everybody would be extra nice to me.

The End.

Arthur smiled. 'That's pretty good!' he said. 'Just what I wanted to say, Shireen.'

'I'm so glad,' said the Askit Basket. 'Bye-bye now!'

Stanley and Arthur called good-bye, and then Prince Haraz plucked the basket out of the air and set it on the desk beside his lamp.

'There! Homework's done,' he said. 'That was an awfully ordinary sort of wish, Stanley. Isn't there something special you've always wanted? Something exciting?'

Stanley knew right away what he wanted most. He had always loved animals; how exciting it would be to have his own zoo! But that would take up too much space, he thought. Just one animal then, a truly unusual pet. A lion? Yes! What fun it would be to walk down the street with a pet lion on a leash!

'I wish for a lion!' he said. 'Real, but friendly.'

'Real, but friendly,' said the genie. 'No problem.'

Stanley realised suddenly that a lion would scare people, and that an elephant would be even greater fun.

'An elephant, I mean!' he shouted. 'Not a lion. An elephant!'

'What?' said Prince Haraz. 'An eleph–? Oh, collibots! Look what you made me do!'

A most unusual head had formed in the air across the room, a head with an elephant's trunk for a nose, but with small, neat, lion-like ears. A lion's mane appeared behind

the head, but then came an elephant's body and legs in a brownish-gold lion colour, and finally a little grey elephant tail with a pretty gold ruff at the tip. All together, these parts made an animal about the size of a medium lion or a small elephant.

'My goodness!' said Stanley. 'What's that?'

'A Liophant.' Prince Haraz sounded annoyed. 'It's your fault, not mine. You overlapped your wish.'

The Liophant opened his mouth wide and went *Grrowll-HONK!* a half roar, half snort that made everyone jump. Then he sat back on his hind legs and went *pant-pant-pant* like a puppy, looking quite nice.

'Well, we got the friendly part right,' said the genie. 'The young ones mostly are.'

Stanley patted him, and Arthur tickled behind the neat little ears. The Liophant licked their hands, and Stanley was not at all sorry that he had mixed up his wish.

Just then, a knock sounded on the bedroom door, and Mrs Lambchop's voice called out, 'Homework done?'

'Come in,' Stanley said, not stopping to think, and the door opened.

'How very quiet you –' Mrs Lambchop began, and then she stopped.

Her eyes moved slowly about the room from Prince Haraz to the Askit Basket, and on to the Liophant.

'Gracious!' she said.

Prince Haraz made a little bow. 'How do you do? You are the mother of these fine lads, I suppose?'

'I am thank you,' said Mrs Lambchop. 'Have we met? I don't seem to –'

'This is Prince Haraz,' Stanley said. 'And that's a Liophant, and that's an Askit Basket.'

'Guess what,' said Arthur. 'Prince Haraz is a genie, and he'll let Stanley have anything he wants.'

'How very generous!' Mrs Lambchop said. 'But I'm not sure . . .' Turning, she called into the living room. 'George, you had better come here! Something quite unexpected has happened.'

'In a moment,' Mr Lambchop called back. 'I am reading an unusual story in my newspaper, about a duck who watches TV.'

'This is even more unusual than that,'

she said, and Mr Lambchop came at once.

'Ah, yes,' he said, looking about the room. 'Yes, I see. Would someone care to explain?'

'I tried to before,' Stanley said. 'Remember? About the lamp, and –'

'Wait, dear,' said Mrs Lambchop.

The Liophant was making snuffling, hungry sounds, so she went off to the kitchen and returned with a large bowl full of hamburger mixed with warm milk. While the Liophant ate, Stanley told what had happened.

'Unusual indeed! And what a fine opportunity for you, Stanley,' Mr Lambchop said when he had heard everything, and then he frowned. 'But I do not approve of using the Askit Basket for homework, boys.

Nor will your teachers, I'm afraid.'

'My plan is, let's not tell them,' Arthur said.

Mr Lambchop gave him a long look. 'Would you take credit for work you have not done?'

Arthur blushed. 'Oh, no! When you put it

that way . . . Gosh, of course not! I wasn't thinking. Because of all the excitement, you know?'

Mr Lambchop wrote NOT IN USE on a piece of cardboard and taped it to the Askit Basket.

'It is too late for any more wishing tonight,' said Mrs Lambchop. 'Prince Haraz, there is a folding bed in the cupboard, so you will be quite comfortable here with Stanley and Arthur. Tomorrow is Saturday, which we Lambchops always spend together in the park. You will join us, I hope?'

'Thank you very much,' said the genie, and he helped Stanley and Arthur set up the bed.

The Liophant was already asleep, and after Mr and Mrs Lambchop had said good night, Mrs Lambchop picked up his bowl. 'Gracious!' she said, putting out the light. 'Three pounds of the best hamburger, and he ate it all!'

It was quite dark in the bedroom, but some moonlight shone through the window.

From their beds, Stanley and Arthur could see that Prince Haraz was still sitting up on his. For a moment they all kept silent, listening to the gentle snoring of the Liophant, and then the genie said, 'Sorry about that. It's having all that nose, probably.'

'It's okay,' Arthur said sleepily. 'Do genies snore?'

'We don't even sleep,' said Prince Haraz. 'Your mother was so kind, I didn't want to tell her. It might have made her feel bad.'

'I'll try to stay awake for a while, if you want to talk,' Stanley said.

'No thanks,' the genie said. 'I'll be fine. After all those years alone in the lamp, it's nice just having company.'

In the Park

Everyone slept late and enjoyed a large breakfast, particularly the Liophant, who ate two more pounds of hamburger, five bananas, and three loaves of bread.

Then, since all the Lambchops enjoyed playing tennis, they set out with their rackets for the courts in the big park close by. Since his genie clothes would make people stare, Prince Haraz borrowed slacks and a shirt from Stanley, and came along to watch.

In the street, they met Ralph Jones, an old college friend of Mr Lambchop's, whom they had not seen for quite some time.

'Nice running into you, George, and you too, Mrs Lambchop,' Mr Jones said. 'Hello, Arthur. Hello, Stanley. Aren't you the one who was flat? Rounded out nicely, I see.'

'You always did have a fine memory, Ralph,' Mr Lambchop said. 'Let me introduce our house guest, Prince Haraz. He is a foreign student, here to study our ways.'

'How do you do,' said the genie. 'I am Fawzi Mustafa Aslan Mirza Melek Namerd Haraz.'

'How do you do,' Mr Jones said. 'Well, I must be on my way. Good-bye, Lambchops. Nice to have met you, Prince Fawzi Mustafa Aslan Mirza Melek Namerd Haraz.'

'He *does* have a wonderful memory,' Mrs Lambchop said, as Mr Jones walked away.

They set out for the park again.

'Wouldn't Mr Jones be surprised if he learned Prince Haraz was a genie?' Mrs Lambchop said. 'The whole world would be amazed. Gracious! We'd all be famous, I'm sure.'

'I was famous once, when I was flat,' Stanley said. 'I didn't like it after a while.'

'I remember,' said Mrs Lambchop. 'Nevertheless, I would enjoy discovering for myself what being famous feels like.'

Prince Haraz looked at Stanley, his eyebrows raised in a questioning way. Stanley gave a little nod, and the genie smiled and nodded back.

Just ahead, near the entrance to the park, was the Famous Museum of Art, one of the most important buildings in the city. A guided-tour bus, filled with visitors from all over the United States and from many foreign countries, had stopped in front of the museum, and the driver was lecturing his passengers through a megaphone.

'Over where those trees are, that's our magnificent City Park!' shouted the driver. 'Here, on the right, is the Famous Museum of Art, with the world's most expensive paintings, statues, and – Oh, what a surprise! We're in luck today, folks!

That's Mrs George Lambchop, coming right toward us! Harriet Lambchop herself, in person! Right there, with the tennis racket!'

Cries of astonishment and pleasure rose from the tourists as they turned in their seats to stare where the driver was pointing.

'What's this?' said Mr Lambchop. 'Is that man talking about you, Harriet?'

'I think so,' said Mrs Lambchop. 'Oh, my goodness! They're coming!'

The tourists were rushing out of the bus, waving cameras and autograph pads. A Japanese family reached Mrs Lambchop first, all with cameras.

'Please, Lambchop lady,' said the husband, bowing politely. 'Honour to take picture, yes?'

'Of course,' said Mrs Lambchop. 'I hope you are enjoying our country. But why *my* picture? I'm not –'

'No, no! Famous, famous! Famous Lambchop lady!' cried the Japanese family, taking pictures as fast as they could.

Mrs Lambchop understood suddenly that her wish had been granted. 'Thank

you, Stanley and Prince Haraz!' she said.
'What fun!'

She posed graciously for all the tourists
and signed dozens of autographs. This took
almost half an hour, and at the entrance to
the park she was recognized again, and had
to do more posing and signing.

It was by now mid-morning, and all the

park's tennis courts were occupied, but the Lambchops' disappointment vanished quickly when they saw a crowd gathered by one court, and learned that Tom McRude, the world's best tennis player, was about to lecture and demonstrate his strokes. Tom McRude had a terrible temper and very bad manners, but because of his wonderful tennis a great many people had come to see him. The Lambchops and Prince Haraz managed to squeeze close to the court, next to the television news cameras that were covering the event.

'None of you can ever be a great tennis player like me,' Tom McRude was saying, out on the court. 'But at least you can have the thrill of getting to see me.'

A little old lady in the crowd gave a tiny

sneeze, and he glared at her. 'What's the matter with you, granny?' he shouted.

The old lady burst into tears, and her friends led her away.

'What a mean fellow!' Prince Haraz whispered to Stanley.

'I can't stand old sneezing people!' said Tom McRude. 'Okay, now I'm going to show how I hit my great forehand! First, I –'

'Hold it, Tom!' called the television director. 'We've just spotted Harriet Lambchop in the crowd here. What a break! Maybe we can get her to say a few words to our audience!'

Even Tom McRude was impressed. '*The* Harriet Lambchop? Here? In person?'

'Swing those cameras this way, fellows!' The director ran to where the Lambchops were standing, and held a microphone out to Mrs Lambchop.

'Wonderful to see you!' he said. 'Everybody wants to know what you think. What about the foreign situation? What's your favourite colour? Go to discos? Do you sleep in pyjamas or a nightdress?'

'Isn't that rather personal?' said Mr Lambchop.

'George, please . . .' Mrs Lambchop smiled at the director. 'Thank you for your kind welcome,' she said into the microphone, 'and I would just like to say at this time that I hope all my fans are having a lovely day here in this delightful park.'

The crowd cheered and waved, and Mrs Lambchop waved back and blew a few kisses. Tom McRude was so jealous of the

attention she was getting that he whacked a tennis ball angrily over the trees behind the court. Noticing, Mrs Lambchop spoke again into the microphone.

'And now,' she said, 'do let us hear what this champion athlete has to tell us about tennis.'

'Yeah!' growled Tom McRude at the TV man. 'Get those cameras back on me!'

When the cameras had swung back to him again, he said, 'Now I want a volunteer, so that I can demonstrate how terrible most players are compared to me.'

Mr Lambchop thought how exciting it would be to venture onto the same court with the champion. Signalling with his racket, he stepped forward.

'Okay.' Tom McRude handed over some balls. 'Let's see how you serve.'

Mr Lambchop prepared to serve.

'He's got his feet wrong!' Tom McRude shouted to the crowd. 'And his grip is wrong! Everything is wrong!'

This made Mr Lambchop so nervous that he served two balls into the net instead of over it.

'Terrible, terrible! Watch how I do it,' said Tom McRude, running to the far side of the court. From there, he served five balls in a row to Mr Lambchop, so hard and fast that Mr Lambchop missed the first four entirely. The fifth one knocked the racket out of his hand.

'Ha, ha!' laughed Tom McRude. 'Now let's see you run!'

He began hitting whizzing forehands and backhands at sharp angles across the court, making Mr Lambchop look very foolish indeed as he raced back and forth, getting redder and redder in the face and missing practically every shot.

The other Lambchops grew very angry as they watched, and Prince Haraz saw how they felt. 'This need not continue, you know,' he whispered to Stanley.

Just then, Mr Lambchop came skidding to a halt before them, banging his knee with his racket as he missed another of the champion's powerful shots.

'Ha, ha! This is how *I* give lessons!' shouted Tom McRude.

Mr Lambchop's eyes met Stanley's, and then he looked at Prince Haraz.

'Okay,' Stanley said, and Prince Haraz smiled his little smile again.

'Thank you,' said Mr Lambchop. Returning to the court, he addressed the crowd. 'Ladies and gentlemen!' he said. 'I will try my serve again!'

Across the net, Tom McRude laughed a nasty laugh and slashed his big racket through the air.

Mr Lambchop served a ball, not into the net this time, but right where it was supposed to go, as fast as a bullet. Tom McRude could only blink as it went past him. Then his mouth fell open. 'Out!' he shouted. 'That ball was out!'

Voices rose from the crowd. 'Shame on you! . . . It was *in*! . . . What a liar! . . . In, in in!'

Tom McRude shook his fist at Mr Lambchop. 'I'll bet you can't do that again!'

Mr Lambchop served three more times, each serve even faster than the first one, and as perfectly placed. Tom McRude could not even touch them, except for the last, which bounced up into his nose.

Then Mr Lambchop began to rally with him, gliding swiftly about the court and returning every shot with ease. With powerful forehands and backhands, he made Tom McRude run from corner to corner; with little drop shots, he drew the champion up to the net, then lobbed marvellous high shots that sent him racing back again. Nobody has ever played such great tennis as Mr Lambchop played that day.

Tom McRude was soon too exhausted, and too angry, to continue. He threw down his racket and jumped on it, and hurled the broken pieces into the net.

'You're just lucky!' he yelled. 'Besides, I have a cold. And the sun was in my eyes the whole time!' He pushed his way through the crowd and ran out of the park.

There was tremendous clapping and cheering for Mr Lambchop, who just smiled modestly and waved his racket in a friendly way. Then he came over to where Stanley and Arthur and Mrs Lambchop and Prince Haraz were standing with the television director.

'You're really *good*,' the director said. 'Frankly, you looked terrible when you first went out there.'

'It takes me a while to get warmed up,' Mr Lambchop said, and led his family away.

In the excitement of the tennis, they had all forgotten Mrs Lambchop's fame, but on the way home she was asked again and again for her autograph, and when they arrived, a photographer and reporter from *Famous Faces* magazine were waiting.

'We want you on the cover of our next issue,' said the photographer.

'I'm supposed to do an interview,' said the reporter. 'Who do you think is sexy? How much do you weigh? Eat health foods? Will there be a movie about your life? Who gave you your first kiss?'

'None of your business!' said Mr Lambchop, and Mrs Lambchop told the

Famous Faces people to go away.

They all watched the evening news on television, hoping Mr Lambchop's amazing tennis would be shown, but only Mrs Lambchop appeared, with Tom McRude in the background. 'The celebrated Harriet Lambchop was in the park today,' said the

newscaster, after which there was a close-up of Mrs Lambchop saying, 'I hope all my fans are having a lovely day,' and that was that.

Mr Lambchop said he didn't care, but he did mind that dinner was interrupted several times by phone calls for Mrs Lambchop from newspaper and magazine and television people. The interruptions didn't bother the Liophant, who ate four pork chops, a jar of peanut butter, a quart of potato salad, and the rubber mat from under his dish.

Chapter Four

The Brothers Fly

'I'm not complaining,' said Arthur, complaining, 'but it's not fair. Some people get to have Liophants and be famous. I want to be President, or as strong as Mighty Man, but all I got was one minute with an Askit Basket I'm not even allowed to use any more.'

He was talking to Stanley and Prince Haraz. It was after dinner, and they were in their bedroom, all in slippers and pyjamas.

'It's not my fault.' Prince Haraz looked hurt. 'A genie just follows orders. Rub, I appear. Wish, I grant. That's it.'

Stanley felt a little sorry for his brother. 'I don't think you ought to be President, Arthur,' he said. 'But I'll wish for you to be the strongest man in the world.' He nodded to Prince Haraz. 'Right now.'

'Oh, good!' Arthur said.

He waited, but nothing happened.

'Darn!' he said, 'I knew it wouldn't work!' Disappointed, he punched his left hand with his right fist.

'Owwww!' Jumping up and down, he waved his hand to relieve the pain.

'When you're the strongest man in the world,' Prince Haraz said, 'you have to be careful what you hit.'

'But I still feel like me,' Arthur said. Testing himself, he took hold of the big desk with one hand and lifted. It rose easily into the air above his head.

Stanley's mouth flew open, and so did the desk drawers. Pencils, paper clips, marbles, and other odds and ends rained down onto the floor.

'Oooops,' Arthur said, and lowered the desk.

'This is ridiculous,' said Prince Haraz, helping him to tidy up. 'The strongest man in the world, in his bedroom picking up desks! Out having adventures, that's where you ought to be.'

'We can't have adventures now,' Arthur said. 'It's almost bedtime.'

Stanley had an idea. 'There'd be time if we could fly! Why can't we all fly somewhere?'

'I've always been able,' said Prince Haraz. 'For you two, it'll take wishing.'

'I wish!' Stanley shouted. 'Flying! Arthur and me both!'

Full of excitement, the brothers held their breath, thinking they would be swept up into the air, but they weren't. After a moment, Arthur tried a few small flapping movements with his elbows.

'Oh, collibots!' said the genie. 'Not like that. Just *think* of flying, and where you want to go.'

It worked.

Stanley and Arthur found themselves suddenly a few feet off the floor, face down

and quite comfortable, and however they wished to go, up or down, forward or back, was the way then went. It was like swimming in soft, invisible water, but without the effort of swimming. After only a few minutes of practice, the brothers were gliding happily about the bedroom, with Prince Haraz giving advice: 'Point your toes, that helps . . . Heads up . . . Good, very good. Yes, I think you're ready now.'

He opened the window and leaned out. 'Nice enough,' he said. 'But there may be coolish winds higher up. We'd better wear something extra.'

Stanley and Arthur put on dressing-gowns and gloves, and the genie borrowed a red parka and a woollen dragon-face ski mask.

'Away we go!' he said, and the brothers floated through the window after him, out into the night.

Up! Up! Up! UP! they went, levelling off now and then to practise speeding, but mostly rising steadily higher. Stanley and Arthur flew side by side, gaining confidence from each other, and the genie kept an eye on them from behind.

It was a beautiful night. The sky above them was full of stars, and the lights of the city, far below, twinkled as brightly as the stars. The brothers' white dressing-gowns shone in the moonlight, and the genie's parka was a glowing red.

They flew above the big park, where an orchestra was giving a concert. Music floated up to them: the clear, sweet tones of flutes and violins and trumpets; the deep, strong notes of cymbals and drums.

'Oh, I'm enjoying this!' Prince Haraz called through his dragon mask. 'So different from inside that lamp!'

They joined hands and circled together, swooping and swaying in time to the music, going round and round above the blaze of light from where the orchestra sat. It was like ice-skating to music at a rink, but much more fun.

In the distance, the blinking wing lights of a big aeroplane moved steadily across the sky.

'Let's chase it!' Stanley shouted.

'Go on! I'll catch up!' Prince Haraz laughed and let them go.

Whoooosh! *Whoooosh*! With their arms by their sides, Stanley and Arthur flashed like rockets across the sky. Their dressing-gowns made little flapping sounds, like the sails of a boat racing before the wind.

The big aeroplane was fast, but the brothers were much faster. When they caught up, they were able to fly all around the plane, looking through the windows at the passengers reading and eating from tiny trays.

Arthur saw a little girl reading a comic

magazine. Zooming in close to her window, he stretched his neck, trying to read over her shoulder. The little girl looked up and saw him. Being mean, she held the magazine down between her knees where he couldn't see it, and then she stuck out her tongue. Arthur stuck his tongue out at her, and the little girl scowled and pulled the curtain across her window.

On the other side of the plane, Stanley saw a young couple with a crying baby across their laps. They looked very tired, but they were being kept awake. Stanley flew up next to the window so that the baby could see him over its parents' shoulders, and then he made a funny face, puffing out his lips and wrinkling his nose. The baby smiled, and Stanley put his thumbs in his ears and wriggled his other fingers. The baby smiled again, and closed its eyes and went to sleep.

Stanley flew around the plane, past the cockpit, to join Arthur on the other side.

There were two pilots in the cockpit, and one of them saw Stanley fly by. Turning his head slowly, he saw both brothers hovering above a wing tip, waiting for Prince Haraz to catch up.

'Guess what I see out there, Bert,' he said.

'The stars in the sky, Max, and below us the mighty ocean,' answered the other pilot.

'No,' said Max. 'Two kids in dressing-gowns.'

'Ha, ha! You are some joker!' said Bert,

but he turned to look.

Only Prince Haraz could be seen now above the wing, his parka flapping as he looked around for Stanley and Arthur, who were hiding from him behind the plane.

'So what do you see, Bert?' asked Max, keeping his own eyes straight ahead. 'Two kids in dressing-gowns, right?'

'Wrong,' said Bert quietly. 'I see a guy in ski clothes with a dragon face.'

The two pilots stared at each other, and then looked out at the wing again, but the genie had flown to join the boys behind the plane.

'Nobody there,' said Max. 'Let's never mention this to anyone, Bert. Okay?'

'Good idea,' Bert answered. 'Definitely.'

They made the plane go faster and had

nothing more to say.

A giant ocean liner, ablaze with lights, made its way across the sea below.

'Come on!' Arthur shouted. He whizzed away, Stanley behind him, and again Prince Haraz laughed and let them go.

The size and beauty of the great ship made the brothers cry out in wonder as they drew near. It was like an enormous birthday cake, each deck a layer sparkling with the brightness of a thousand candles.

'Look, Stanley!' Arthur pointed. 'They're having a big party on the main deck!'

They flew closer to enjoy the fun, and then they saw that it was not a party, but a robbery.

The main deck was crowded because masked robbers had lined up all the passengers, and were taking their money and jewellery and watches. The helicopter in which the robbers had landed was parked just below the captain's bridge, which overlooked the main deck. The captain and the other ship's officers had been chained up on the bridge. They had struggled, but now there was nothing they could do.

'We've got to help, Stanley!' Arthur said.

He zoomed down to the bridge, and shouted over the railing at the robbers on the deck below. 'Stop, you crooks! Give back all that money and jewellery and other stuff!'

Using his great strength, Arthur tore away the ropes and chains that bound the ship's officers. It was as easy for him as if he were tearing up paper.

The robbers were amazed. Unable to believe their eyes, they stumbled back from their victims, dropping money and jewellery all over the deck.

'Oh, lordy!' one robber yelled. 'Who are you?'

Remembering his favourite comic-magazine hero, Arthur could not resist showing off. He flew ten feet up in the air and stayed there, looking fierce.

'I am Mighty Arthur!' he shouted in a deep voice. 'Mighty Arthur, Enemy of Crime!'

Exclamations rose from the robbers and passengers and ship's officers. 'So strong, and a flier too! . . . Who expected Mighty Arthur? . . . Are we ever lucky! . . . This ought to be on TV!'

Now Stanley came swooping down from

the sky with his dressing-gown belt untied,
so that the gown flared behind him like
a cape.

'And I'm Mighty Stanley!' he called.
'Defender of the Innocent!'

'I do that too!' cried Arthur, wishing he
had made his robe a cape. 'We both do

good things, but I'm the really strong one!'

Several robbers were trying to escape in the helicopter, and he saw another chance to prove his strength.

The helicopter was already rising, but Arthur flashed through the air until he was directly above it, and with one hand he pushed it back onto the deck. When the frightened robbers jumped out, the ship's officers grabbed them and tied them up.

Now the passengers were even more excited and amazed. 'Did you see that?' they said, and 'Mighty Arthur and Mighty Stanley, both on the same day!' and 'This is *better* than TV!'

The brothers flew up to join Prince Haraz, who had been circling over the ship. 'What a pair of show-offs!' said the genie, as they set out for home. 'Even worse than I used to be.'

Behind them, cheers floated up from the grateful passengers and crew. 'Hooray for our rescuers!' they heard, and 'Especially Mighty Arthur!' which was followed a moment later by 'Mighty Stanley too, of course!'

Soon the big ship was no more than an outline of tiny lights in the black sea below, and the last cheer was only a whisper above the rushing of the wind. 'Three cheers . . . for . . . the Enemy . . . of . . . Crime . . . and the . . . Defender . . . of the Inno . . . cent!'

The brothers felt very proud, but it had been a tiring adventure, and they were not sorry when the city came into sight.

Chapter Five

The Last Wish

When the three adventurers flew back into
the bedroom, the Liophant was just finishing
an enormous bowl of spaghetti mixed with
chocolate cookies and milk. He looked
sleepy, but Mr and Mrs Lambchop, standing
by the door, were very much awake.

'Thank goodness you are all right!' Mrs
Lambchop ran to hug her sons.

Mr Lambchop's voice was stern. 'Where

have you been? Is that you, Prince Haraz, behind that dragon face?'

The genie took off his ski mask. 'Were you worried?' he said. 'Sorry. We just went for a little flight.'

'Wait till you hear!' said Arthur. 'You can't tell from looking, but I'm the strongest man in the world, and –'

'First take off those dressing-gowns and gloves,' said Mrs Lambchop. 'It is not wise to get overheated.'

She went on talking while they put their things away. 'What a *dreadful* evening! The phone never stopped ringing. I was asked to go on six television shows, and to be in an advertisement for a new kind of soap – they wanted pictures of me in the bathtub, so of course I said no! – and to sit with the mayor during the next parade. I'm exhausted! And such a fright, after all that, to find the window open and the three of you gone!'

'We thought we'd be right back,' said Stanley, apologising. 'We didn't know so many exciting things would happen.'

Everyone sat down, and he explained about wishing Arthur strong, and the flying, not leaving out how they had chased the aeroplane and startled the robbers on the great ship at sea. Mr and Mrs Lambchop looked more and more worried as they listened, and when Stanley was done, Mr Lambchop gave a deep sigh.

'It seems, Prince Haraz,' he said, 'that there are often unexpected consequences when wishes come true.'

The genie nodded. 'I'll say. That's how I

got myself put into a lamp.'

'It is not just the difficulty about the Askit Basket,' Mr Lambchop said. 'Mrs Lambchop has been famous for only a day, and already it has exhausted her and cost our family its privacy. And though Tom McRude deserved the lessons he got, his tennis comes from natural ability, and I am not proud of having shamed him by the use of magic.'

'And now Arthur is so strong that other

boys will be afraid to play with him,' said
Mrs Lambchop. 'And this flying, and
getting mixed up with criminals – Oh, it
is worrying!'

'Indeed it is,' Mr Lambchop said. 'We must
all think hard about what has happened, and
what the future may bring.'

'I will make hot chocolate,' said Mrs
Lambchop. 'It is extremely helpful when
there is serious thinking to be done.'

Everyone enjoyed the delicious hot chocolate she brought from the kitchen, with a marshmallow for each cup. Mr and Mrs Lambchop and Stanley and Arthur sat with their eyes half closed, sipping and thinking. Prince Haraz kept silent for a while, and then he said he was sorry to have caused problems, and began to pace up and down. The Liophant went to sleep.

At last Mr Lambchop put down his cup and cleared his throat. 'May I have your attention, please?' he said.

When they were all looking at him, he said, 'Here is my opinion. Genies and their magic, Prince Haraz, may be well suited to faraway lands and long-ago times, but the Lambchops have always been quite ordinary people, and this is the United States of

America, and the time is today. We are grateful, I'm sure, for the excitement you have brought us, but I now believe that it would have been better for everyone if you had remained in your lamp. And so I must ask: Is it possible for Stanley to unwish the wishes he has made?'

'There is a way, actually,' said Prince Haraz, looking surprised.

Mrs Lambchop clapped her hands. 'How very wise you are, George! Don't you agree, boys?'

Arthur wasn't sure. 'I really like the flying,' he said, and then he sighed. 'But being so strong . . . I guess nobody *would* play with me.'

'What I care most about is the Liophant,' Stanley said. 'Couldn't we just keep him?'

'He *is* very lovable,' Mrs Lambchop said. 'But he *eats* so much! We cannot afford to keep him.'

'Sad, my dear, but true,' said Mr Lambchop. 'Now tell us, Prince Haraz, how we are to proceed.'

'It's called Reverse Wishing,' said the genie.

The little green lamp was still on the desk, and he picked it up and turned it over. 'The instructions should be right here,' he said. 'Let's see . . .'

The Lambchops waited anxiously as he studied the words that had been carved into the bottom of the lamp.

'Simple enough,' he said, after a moment. 'Each wish has to be reversed separately. I just say "Mandrono!" and –' His voice rose.

'Oh, collibots! Double florts! See that little circle there? This is a training lamp! There may not be enough wishes left!'

'What?' exclaimed Mr Lambchop. 'What's a training lamp?'

'They're used for beginners like me, so we don't do too much for one person,' Prince Haraz said unhappily. 'The number in the circle, the fifteen, that's all the wishes I'm allowed to grant Stanley.'

The Lambchops all spoke at once. 'What? ... Only fifteen? ... You never said! ... Oh dear!'

'Please, I'm embarrassed enough,' said the genie, very red in the face. 'A training lamp! As if I were a baby!'

'We are all beginners at one time or another,' Mr Lambchop said. 'What matters now is, are fifteen wishes enough?'

Prince Haraz counted, folding his fingers to be sure he got it right. 'Askit Basket, Liophant – lucky he doesn't count double – that's two, and fame for Mrs Lambchop and the fancy tennis, that's four. Making Arthur strong, five, and flying for him *and* Stanley is two more . . .' He smiled. 'Seven, and seven for the reversing is fourteen! And we have a wish left over for some sort of goodbye treat!'

'Thank goodness!' said Mrs Lambchop. 'Could you manage all the reversing right now, please? It has grown very late.'

'I'll do the whole family in a bunch,' said the genie. 'Let's see. . . . Strength, famous, tennis, two flying. Ready, Arthur? No more Mighty Man after this, I'm afraid.'

'Will I feel weak?' Arthur asked. 'Will I flop over?'

The genie shook his head. 'Mandrono!' he said. 'Mandrono, Mandrono, Mandrono, Mandrono!'

Arthur felt a curious but not unpleasant prickling on the back of his neck. When the prickling stopped, he gave the big desk a shove, but it didn't move.

'I'm just the regular me again,' he said. 'Oh, well.'

'And I am just Harriet Lambchop again,' said Mrs Lambchop, smiling. 'An unimportant person.'

'To all of us, my dear, you are the most important person we know,' Mr Lambchop said. 'Arthur, you are as strong as you were yesterday. Think of it that way.'

Prince Haraz sipped the last of his hot chocolate. 'Where was I? Oh, yes . . .' He glanced at the Askit Basket, said, 'Mandrono!' and the basket was gone. 'That leaves just the Liophant,' he said.

The Lambchops all turned to look at the Liophant who was awake now and sitting up in the corner, trying to scratch behind his lion ears with the tip of his elephant trunk. Stanley went over and patted him, and the Liophant licked his hand.

'How sweet!' said Mrs Lambchop. 'George, perhaps . . .?'

'What makes Liophants happiest,' the genie said, 'is open spaces, and chasing unicorns, and wrestling with other Liophants.'

'Then send him where it's like that,' said Stanley, patting again. The Liophant

vanished halfway through the pat.

For a moment no one spoke. Then Mr Lambchop put his hand on Stanley's shoulder in a sympathetic way. 'Good for you,' he said.

Stanley sat down to think about the one wish he had left, and Mrs Lambchop began to collect the hot chocolate cups. 'Where will you go, Prince Haraz, when you leave us?' she asked.

'Right back into that stuffy little lamp,' said the genie. 'And then it's just wait, wait, wait! Another thousand years, at least. It's a punishment I got for playing too many tricks. My friends warned me, but I wouldn't listen.'

Sighing, he handed Mrs Lambchop his empty cup. 'Mosef, Ali, Ben Sifa, little Fawz. Such wonderful fellows! I think of them when I'm alone in the lamp, the fun they must be having, the games, the freedom . . .'

The genie's voice trembled, and he turned his head away. All the Lambchops felt very sorry for him.

Then Arthur had an idea. He ran across

the room to whisper it to Stanley.

'Whispering?' said Mrs Lambchop. 'Where are your manners, dear?'

'Who cares?' Prince Haraz said crossly. 'Let's have that last wish, and I'll smoke back into my lamp.'

The brothers were smiling at each other.

'Good idea, right?' said Arthur.

'Oh, yes!' Stanley said.

He turned to the genie. 'Here is my last wish, Prince Haraz. I wish for you not to stay in the lamp, but to go back where you came from, so that you can be with your genie friends and have good times with them, forever from now on!'

Prince Haraz gasped. His mouth fell open.

Mr Lambchop worried that he might faint.

'Are you all right?' he asked. 'Is Stanley not allowed to set you free?'

'Oh, yes . . .' The genie's voice was very low. 'It's allowed. But whoever heard of . . . That is, nobody ever used up a wish for the sake of a genie. Not until now.'

'How very selfish people can be!' said Mrs Lambchop.

Prince Haraz rubbed his eyes. 'What a fine family this is!' he said, beginning to smile. 'I thank you all. The name of Lambchop will be honoured always, wherever genies meet.'

His smile enormous now, he shook hands with each of the Lambchops. The last shake was with Stanley, and the genie was already a bit smoky about the edges. By the time he let go of Stanley's hand, he was all smoke,

a dark cloud that swirled briefly over the little lamp on the desk, and then poured in through the spout until not a puff remained.

Full of wonder, the Lambchops gathered

about the lamp, and after a moment Arthur put his lips to the spout.

'Good-bye, Prince Haraz!' he called. 'Have a nice trip!'

From inside the lamp, faint and far away, a voice cried, 'Bless you, bless you all . . .' and then there was only silence in the room.

'I am proud of you, Stanley,' Mr Lambchop said. 'Your last wish was generous and kind.'

'It was my idea, actually,' Arthur said, and Mrs Lambchop kissed the top of his head.

Then she gathered the last of the hot chocolate cups and put them on her tray. 'Off to bed now,' she said. 'Tomorrow is another day.'

Stanley and Arthur got into bed, and she turned out the light.

'The lamp was supposed to be a surprise birthday present,' Stanley said sleepily. 'Now it won't be a surprise anymore.'

'I will love my present when you give it to me,' said Mrs Lambchop. 'And Prince Haraz was a tremendous surprise. Good night, boys.'

She kissed them both, and so did Mr Lambchop, and they went out.

The brothers lay quietly in the darkness for a while, and then Stanley sighed. 'I miss the Liophant a little,' he said. 'But I don't mind about the rest.'

'Me neither,' Arthur yawned. 'Florts, Stanley, and good night.'

'Good night,' Stanley said. 'Collibots.'

'Mandrono,' murmured Arthur, and soon they were both asleep.

FLAT STANLEY

Invisible Stanley

Prologue

Stanley Lambchop spoke into the darkness above his bed. 'I can't sleep. It's the rain, I think.'

There was no response from the bed across the room.

'I'm hungry too,' Stanley said. 'Are you awake, Arthur?'

'I am now,' said his younger brother. 'You woke me.'

Stanley fetched an apple from the kitchen, and ate it by the bedroom window. The rain had worsened.

'I'm still hungry,' he said.

'Raisins . . . shelf . . .' murmured Arthur, half asleep again.

Crash! came thunder. Lightning flashed.

Stanley found the little box of raisins on a shelf by the window. He ate one.

Crash! *Flash*!

Stanley ate more raisins.

Crash! *Flash*!

Arthur yawned. 'Go to bed. You can't be hungry still.'

'I'm not, actually.' Stanley got back into bed. 'But I feel sort of . . . Oh, *different*, I guess.'

He slept.

Where is Stanley?

'Breakfast is ready, George. We must wake the boys,' Mrs Lambchop said to her husband.

Just then Arthur Lambchop called from the bedroom he shared with his brother.

'Hey! Come here! Hey!'

Mr and Mrs Lambchop smiled, recalling another morning that had begun like this. An enormous bulletin board, they had discovered, had fallen on Stanley during the night, leaving him unhurt but no more than half an inch thick. And so he had remained until Arthur blew him round again, weeks later, with a bicycle pump.

'Hey!' a call came again. 'Are you coming? Hey!'

Mrs Lambchop held firm views about good manners and correct speech. 'Hay is for horses, not people, Arthur,' she said as they entered the bedroom. 'As well you know.'

'Excuse me,' said Arthur. 'The thing is, I can *hear* Stanley, but I can't *find* him!'

Mr and Mrs Lambchop looked about the room. A shape was visible beneath the covers of Stanley's bed, and the pillow was squashed down, as if a head rested upon it. But there was no head.

'Why are you staring?' The voice was
Stanley's.

Smiling, Mr Lambchop looked under
the bed, but saw only a pair of slippers and
an old tennis ball. 'Not here,' he said.

Arthur put out a hand, exploring.
'Ouch!' said Stanley's voice. 'You poked
my nose!'

Arthur gasped.

Mrs Lambchop stepped forward. 'If I may . . .?' Gently, using both hands, she felt about.

A giggle rose from the bed. 'That *tickles*!'

'Oh, my!' said Mrs Lambchop.

She looked at Mr Lambchop and he at

her, as they had during past great surprises. Stanley's flatness had been the first of these. Another had come the evening they discovered a young genie, Prince Haraz, in the bedroom with Stanley and Arthur, who had summoned him accidentally from a lamp.

Mrs Lambchop drew a deep breath. 'We must face facts, George. Stanley is now invisible.'

'You're *right!*' said a startled voice from the bed. 'I can't see my feet! Or my pyjamas!'

'Darndest thing I've ever seen,' said Mr Lambchop. 'Or *not* seen, I should say. Try some other pyjamas, Stanley.'

Stanley got out of bed, and put on different pyjamas, but these too vanished, reappearing when he took them off. It was the same with the shirt and slacks he tried next.

'Gracious!' Mrs Lambchop shook her head. 'How are we to keep *track* of you, dear?'

'I know!' said Arthur. Untying a small red balloon, a party favour, that floated

10

above his bed, he gave Stanley the string to hold. 'Try this,' he said.

The string vanished, but not the balloon.

'There!' said Mrs Lambchop. 'At least we can tell, approximately, where Stanley is. Now let's all have breakfast. Then, George, we must see what Doctor Dan makes of this.'

Doctor Dan

'What's that red balloon doing here?' said
Doctor Dan. 'Well, never mind. Good
morning, Mr and Mrs Lambchop.
Something about Stanley, my nurse says.
He's not been taken flat again?'

'No, no,' said Mrs Lambchop. 'Stanley
has remained round.'

'They mostly do,' said Doctor Dan.
'Well, let's have the little fellow in.'

'I am in,' said Stanley, standing directly before him. 'Holding the balloon.'

'Ha, ha, Mr Lambchop!' said Doctor Dan. 'You are an excellent ventriloquist! But I see through your little joke!'

'What you see through,' said Mr Lambchop, 'is Stanley.'

'Beg pardon?' said Doctor Dan.

'Stanley became invisible during the night,' Mrs Lambchop explained. 'We are quite unsettled by it.'

'Head ache?' Doctor Dan asked Stanley's balloon. 'Throat sore? Stomach upset?'

'I feel fine,' Stanley said.

'I see. Hmmmm . . .' Doctor Dan shook his head. 'Frankly, despite my long years of practice, I've not run into this before. But one of my excellent medical books, *Difficult and Peculiar Cases*, by

14

Doctor Franz Gemeister, may help.'

He took a large book from the shelf behind him and looked into it.

'Ah! "Disappearances", page 134.' He found the page. 'Hmmmm . . . Not much here, I'm afraid. France, 1851: a Madame Poulenc vanished while eating bananas in the rain. Spain, 1923: the Gonzales twins, aged 11, became invisible after eating fruit salad. Lightning had been observed. The most recent case, 1968, is Oombok, an Eskimo chief, last seen eating canned peaches during a blizzard.'

Doctor Dan returned the book to the shelf.

'That's all,' he said. 'Gemeister suspects a connection between bad weather and fruit.'

'It stormed last night,' said Stanley. 'And I ate an apple. Raisins, too.'

'There you are,' said Doctor Dan. 'But we must look at the bright side, Mr and Mrs Lambchop. Stanley seems perfectly healthy, except for the visibility factor. We'll just keep an eye on him.'

'Easier said than done,' said Mr Lambchop. 'Why do his *clothes* also disappear?'

'Not my field, I'm afraid,' said Doctor Dan. 'I suggest a textile specialist.'

'We've kept you long enough, doctor,' Mrs Lambchop said. 'Come, George, Stanley – Where *are* you, Stanley? Ah! Just hold the balloon a bit higher, dear. Goodbye, Doctor Dan.'

★ ★ ★

By dinner time, Mr and Mrs Lambchop and Arthur had become quite sad. The red balloon, though useful in locating Stanley, kept reminding them of how much they missed his dear face and smile.

But after dinner, Mrs Lambchop, who was artistically talented, replaced the red balloon with a pretty white one and got out her watercolour paints. Using four colours and several delicate brushes, she painted an excellent likeness of Stanley, smiling, on the white balloon.

Everyone became at once more cheerful. Stanley said he felt almost his old self again, especially when he looked in the mirror.

The First Days

The next morning Mrs Lambchop wrote a note to Stanley's teacher, tied a stronger string to his balloon, and sent him off to school.

Dear Miss Benchley, the note said. *Stanley has unexpectedly become invisible. You will find the balloon a useful guide to his presence.*

Sincerely, Harriet Lambchop

★ ★ ★

Miss Benchley spoke to the class. 'We must not stare at where we suppose Stanley to be,' she said. 'And not gossip about his state.'

Nevertheless, word soon reached a newspaper. A reporter visited the school and wrote a story for his paper.

The headline read: 'Smiling Student: Once You Saw Him, Now You Don't!' Beneath it were two photographs, a *Before* and an *After*.

The *Before*, taken by Miss Benchley a week earlier, showed a smiling Stanley at his desk. For the *After*, taken by the reporter, Stanley had posed the same way, but only the desk and his smiley-face balloon, bobbing above it, could be seen. The story included a statement by Miss

Benchley that Stanley was in fact at the desk and, to the best of her knowledge, smiling.

Mr and Mrs Lambchop bought several copies of the paper for out-of-town friends. Her colourful balloon artwork lost something in black and white, Mrs Lambchop said, but on the whole it had photographed well.

Arthur said that *Invisible Boy's Brother* would have been an interesting picture, and that Stanley should suggest it if the reporter came round again.

Being invisible offered temptations, Mr and Mrs Lambchop said, but Stanley must resist them. It would be wrong to spy on people, for example, or sneak up to hear what they were saying.

But the next Saturday afternoon, when the Lambchops went to the movies, it was Arthur who could not resist.

'Don't buy a seat for Stanley,' he whispered at the ticket window. 'Just hide his balloon. Who'd know?'

'That would be deceitful, dear,' said Mrs Lambchop. 'Four seats, please,' she told the ticket lady. 'We want one for our coats, you see.'

'Wasn't *that* deceitful, sort of?' Arthur asked, as they went in.

'Not the same way,' said Mr Lambchop, tucking Stanley's balloon beneath his seat.

Just as the film began, a very tall man sat directly in front of Stanley, blocking his view. Mr Lambchop took Stanley on his lap, from which the screen was easily seen, and the people farther back saw right

through him without knowing it. Stanley greatly enjoyed the show.

'See?' said Arthur, as they went out. 'Stanley didn't even *need* a seat.'

'You have a point,' said Mr Lambchop, whose legs had gone to sleep.

In the Park

It was Sunday afternoon. Arthur had gone to visit a friend, so Mr and Mrs Lambchop set out with Stanley for a nearby park. The streets were crowded, and Stanley carried his balloon, to lessen the risk of being jostled by people hurrying by.

Near the park, they met Ralph Jones, an old college friend of Mr Lambchop's.

'Always a treat running into your family,

George!' said Mr Jones. 'The older boy was flat once, I recall. You had him rolled up. And once you had a foreign student with you. A prince, yes?'

'What a memory you have!' said Mr Lambchop, remembering that he had introduced as a 'foreign student' the young genie with them at the time.

'How are you, Ralph?' said Mrs Lambchop.

'Stanley? Say hello to Mr Jones.'

'Take care!' said Mr Jones. 'That balloon is floating – Hmmmm . . . Just where *is* Stanley?'

'Holding the balloon,' Stanley said. 'I got invisible somehow.'

'Is that so? First flat, now invisible.' Ralph Jones shook his head. 'Kids! Always one thing or another, eh, George? My oldest needs dental work. Well, I must run! Say hello to that prince, if he's still visiting. Prince Fawzi Mustafa Aslan Mirza Melek Namerd Haraz, as I recall.'

'A truly *remarkable* memory,' said Mrs Lambchop, as Mr Jones walked away.

By a field in the park, the Lambchops found a bench on which to rest.

On the field, children were racing bicycles, round and round. Suddenly, shouts rose. 'Give up, Billy! Billy's no good! Billy, Billy, silly Billy, he can't ride a bike!'

'That must be Billy,' said Mrs Lambchop. 'The little fellow, so far behind the rest. Oh, dear! How he teeters!'

Stanley remembered how nervous he had been when he was learning to ride, and how his father had steadied him. Poor Billy! If only – I'll do it! he thought, and tied his balloon to the bench.

When Billy came round again, Stanley darted across the field. Taking hold of the teetering bicycle from behind, he began to run.

'Uh-oh!' said little Billy, surprised to be gaining speed.

Stanley ran harder, keeping the bicycle steady. The pedals rose and fell, faster and faster, then faster still.

'Yikes!' cried Billy.

Stanley ran as fast as he could. Soon they passed the boy riding ahead, then another boy, and another! Not until they had passed all the other riders did Stanley, now out of breath, let go.

'Wheeee!' shouted Billy, and went round once more by himself.

'You win, Billy!' shouted the other boys.

'How did you get so good? And so *suddenly*! . . . You sure had us fooled!'

Stanley got his breath back and returned to Mr and Mrs Lambchop on the bench.

'Too bad you missed it, Stanley,' said Mr Lambchop, pretending he had not guessed the truth. 'That teetery little boy, he suddenly rode very well.'

'Oh?' said Stanley, pretending also. 'I wasn't paying attention, I guess.'

Mr Lambchop gave him a little poke in the ribs.

★ ★ ★

Half an hour passed, and Mrs Lambchop worried that they might sit too long in the sun. In Stanley's present state, she said, over-tanning would be difficult to detect.

Just then a young man and a pretty girl strolled past, hand in hand, and halted in a grove close by.

'That is Phillip, the son of my dear friend, Mrs Hodgson,' Mrs Lambchop said. 'And the girl must be his sweetheart, Lucia. Such a sad story! They are in love, and Phillip wants very much to propose marriage. But he is too shy. He tries and tries, Mrs Hodgson says, but each time his courage fails. And Lucia is too timid to coax the proposal from him.'

Mr Lambchop was not the least bit shy. 'I'll go introduce myself,' he said. 'And pop the question for him.'

'No, George.' Mrs Lambchop shook her head. 'Lucia must hear the words from his own lips.'

An idea came to Stanley.

'Be right back!' he said, and ran to the grove in which the young couple stood. Beside them, he stood very still.

'. . . nice day, Lucia, don't you think?' Phillip was saying. 'Though they say it may rain. Who knows?'

'You are quite right, I'm sure, Phillip,' the girl replied. 'I do value your opinions about the weather.'

'You are kind, very kind.' Phillip trembled a bit. 'Lucia, I want to ask . . . I mean . . . Would you . . . Consent, that is . . .' He gulped. 'What a pretty dress you have!'

'Thank you,' said Lucia. 'I like your necktie. You were saying, Phillip?'

'Ah!' said Phillip. 'Right! Yes! I want . . .'
He bit his lip. 'Look! A dark cloud, there
in the west! It may rain after all.'

'I hope not.' Lucia seemed close to tears.
'I mean, if it rained . . . Well, we might
get wet.'

This is *very* boring, Stanley thought.

The conversation grew even more
boring. Again and again, Phillip failed to
declare his love, chatting instead about the
weather, or the look of a tree, or children
playing in the park.

'I want to ask, dear Lucia,' Phillip began
again, for perhaps the twentieth time, 'if
you will . . . That is . . . If you . . . If . . .'

'Yes?' said Lucia, for perhaps the
twentieth time. '*What*, Phillip? *What* do
you wish to say?'

Stanley leaned forward.

'Lucia . . . ?' said Phillip. 'Hmmmm . . .
Ah! I . . .'

'*Marry me!*' said Stanley, making his
voice as much like Phillip's as he could.

Lucia's eyes opened wide. 'I *will*,
Phillip!' she cried. 'Of course I will
marry you!'

Phillip looked as if he might faint.
'What? Did I – ? You *will*?'

Lucia hugged him, and they kissed.

'I've proposed at last!' cried Phillip.

'I can hardly believe I spoke the words!'

You didn't, Stanley thought.

Mr and Mrs Lambchop had seen the lovers embrace. 'Well done, Stanley!' they said when he returned to their bench, and several more times on the way home.

Mrs Hodgson called that evening to report that Phillip and Lucia would soon be wed. 'How wonderful!' Mrs Lambchop said. She had glimpsed them in the park just that afternoon. Such a handsome pair! So much in love!

Stanley teased her. 'You said never to sneak up on people, or spy on them. But I did today. Are you mad at me?'

'Oh, very angry,' said Mrs Lambchop, and kissed the top of his head.

The TV Show

Arthur was feeling left out. 'Stanley always gets to have interesting adventures,' he said. 'And that newspaper story was just about *him*. Nobody seems interested in *me*.'

'The best way to draw attention, dear,' said Mrs Lambchop, 'is by one's character. Be kindly. And fair. Cheerfulness is much admired, as is wit.'

'I can't manage all that,' said Arthur.

Mrs Lambchop spoke privately to Stanley. 'Your brother is a bit jealous,' she said.

'When I was flat, Arthur was jealous because people stared at me,' Stanley said. 'Now they can't see me at all, and he's jealous again.'

Mrs Lambchop sighed. 'If you can find a way to cheer him, do.'

The very next day an important TV person telephoned Mr Lambchop.

'Teddy Talker here, Lambchop,' he said. 'Host of the enormously popular TV chat show, "Talking With Teddy Talker". Will Stanley appear on it?'

'It would please us to have Stanley *appear* anywhere at all,' Mr Lambchop said.

'People can't see him, you know.'

'I'll just say he's there,' said Teddy Talker. 'Speak to the boy. Let me know.'

Stanley said that he did not particularly care to go on TV. But then he remembered about cheering up Arthur.

'All right,' he said. 'But Arthur too. He likes to tell jokes and do magic tricks. Say we'll *both* be on the show.'

Arthur was very pleased, and that evening the brothers planned what they would do. The next morning, Mr Lambchop told Teddy Talker.

'Excellent plan!' said the TV man. 'This Friday, yes? Thank you, Lambchop!'

'Welcome, everybody!' said Teddy Talker that Friday evening, from the stage of his TV theatre. 'Wonderful guests tonight!

Including an invisible boy!'

In the front row, applauding with the rest of the audience, Mr and Mrs Lambchop thought of Stanley and Arthur, waiting now in a dressing-room backstage. How excited they must be!

The other guests were already seated on the sofa by Teddy Talker's desk. He chatted first with a lady who had written a book about sausage, then with a tennis

champion who had become a rabbi, then with a very pretty young woman who had won a beauty contest, but planned now to devote herself to the cause of world peace.

At last came the announcement that began the Lambchop plan.

'Invisible Stanley has been delayed, but will be here shortly,' Teddy Talker told the audience. 'Meanwhile, we are fortunate in having with us his very talented brother!'

Protests rose. 'Brother? A *visible* brother? . . . Drat! . . . Good thing we got in free!'

'Ladies and gentlemen!' said Teddy Talker. 'Mirth and Magic with Arthur Lambchop!'

Arthur stepped out on to the stage, wearing a smart black magician's cape Mrs Lambchop had made for him, and carrying a small box, which he placed on Teddy Talker's desk.

'Hello, everybody!' he said. 'The box is for later. Now let's have fun! Heard the story about the three holes in the ground?' He waited, smiling. 'Well, well, well!'

Two people laughed, but that was all.

'I don't understand,' said a lady sitting behind Mr and Mrs Lambchop.

Mr Lambchop turned in his seat. 'A "well" is a hole in the ground,' he said.

'"Well, well, well." Three holes.'

'Ah! I see!' said the lady.

'A riddle, ladies and gentlemen!' cried Arthur. 'Where do kings keep their armies?'

'Where?' someone called.

'In their sleevies!' said Arthur.

Many people laughed now, including the lady who had missed the first joke. 'I *got* that one,' she said.

'And now a mind-reading trick!' Arthur announced. He shuffled a deck of cards, and let Teddy Talker draw one.

'Don't let me see it!' he said. 'But look at it! Picture it in your mind! I will concentrate, using my magic powers!' Arthur closed his eyes. 'Hmmm . . . hmmm . . . Your card, sir, is the four of hearts!'

'It is!' cried Teddy Talker. 'It *is* the four of hearts!'

Voices rose again. 'Incredible! . . . He can read minds? . . . So young, too! . . . Do that one again, lad!'

'Certainly!' said Arthur.

But he had used a false deck in which *every* card was the four of hearts, and the audience would surely guess if that card were named again. Fortunately, the brothers had thought of this. Backstage, Stanley tied his balloon to a chair.

Arthur now shuffled a real deck of cards, then called for a volunteer. When an elderly gentleman came on to the stage, Stanley tiptoed out to stand behind him. The audience applauded the volunteer. How peculiar this is! Stanley thought. Hundreds of people looking, but no one can see me!

'Draw a card, sir!' said Arthur. 'Thank you!

48

Keep it hidden! But picture it in your mind!' Again closing his eyes, he pretended to be thinking hard.

A quick peek told Stanley that the volunteer held the ten of clubs. Tiptoeing over, he whispered in his brother's ear.

Arthur opened his eyes. 'I have it. The card is – The ten of clubs!'

'Yes! Bravo!' cried the old gentleman. The audience clapped hard as he returned to his seat.

Mr Lambchop smiled at the lady behind him. 'Our son,' he said.

'So clever!' said the lady. 'What *will* he do next?'

Mrs Lambchop drew a deep breath. That morning, Stanley and Arthur had borrowed a pet frog from the boy next door. What came next, she knew, would be the most daring part of the evening's plan!

'Ladies and gentlemen!' said Arthur. 'A new kind of magic! Arthur Lambchop – that's me! – and Henry, the Air-Dancing Frog!'

He lifted Henry from the box on Teddy Talker's desk, and held him up. Henry, who appeared to be smiling, wore a little white shirt with an 'H' on it, made by Mrs Lambchop along with Arthur's cape.

'Fly, Henry!' cried Arthur. 'Fly out, and stand still in the air!'

Stepping forward, Stanley took Henry from Arthur's hands and ran to the far side of the stage. Here he stopped, holding the frog high above his head. Henry wriggled his legs.

'Amazing!' shouted the audience. 'Who'd

believe it? . . . That's some frog! . . . What keeps him up there?'

'Circle, Henry!' Arthur commanded. 'Circle in the air!'

Stanley walked rapidly in circles, swaying Henry as he went.

The audience was tremendously impressed. 'What a fine magician! . . . Mind reading *and* frog flying! . . . You don't see that every day!'

Pretending to control Henry's flight, Arthur kept a finger pointed as Stanley swooped the frog all about the stage. 'Whoops!' cried Teddy Talker as Henry flew above his desk. On the long sofa, the sausage writer and tennis rabbi and the beauty contest winner ducked down. Even Mr and Mrs Lambchop, knowing the secret of Henry's flight, thought it an amazing sight.

At last, to great applause, Arthur took Henry into his own hands and returned him to the little box.

Stanley tiptoed off to get his smiley-face balloon. The plan now called for Teddy Talker to announce the arrival of the invisible boy, and introduce him.

But Arthur had stepped forward again.

'Thank you for cheering me,' he told the audience. 'But I have to say something. That first mind-reading trick, I really did do that one. But the second trick – Actually, I can't read minds at all. And the flying frog, he –'

Voices rose. 'Can't read minds? . . . We've been lied to! . . . The *frog* was lying? . . . Not the frog, stupid! . . . Wait, he's not done!'

'Please! Listen!' said Arthur. 'It wouldn't

be fair to let you think I did everything by myself. I had a helper! The second trick, he saw the card and told me what it was. And Henry . . . Well, my helper was whooshing him in the air!'

By now the audience was terribly confused. 'Who? . . . What helper? . . . It was just a regular frog? . . . But *some* frogs fly! . . . No, squirrels, not frogs! . . . *Whooshing?*'

Arthur went on. 'My brother Stanley helped me! He fixed it for me to be on this show! He's a really nice brother, and I thank him a lot!'

Teddy Talker had sprung to his feet. 'Ladies and gentlemen! May I present now a very special guest, who has been here all along! The invisible boy! Stanley Lambchop!'

Stanley came on to the stage, carrying his smiley-face balloon. Arthur put out

his hand, and the audience could tell that Stanley had taken it. There was tremendous applause.

The brothers bowed again and again, Stanley's balloon bobbing up and down. Arthur's smile was plain to see, and Mr and Mrs Lambchop, as they applauded, thought that even the balloon's painted smile seemed brighter than before.

'I have two children myself,' said the lady behind them. 'Both entirely visible, and without theatrical flair. We are a very *usual* family.'

'As we are,' said Mr Lambchop, smiling. 'Mostly, that is.'

Arthur left the stage, and Stanley sat on the sofa between the sausage writer and the beauty contest winner and answered Teddy Talker's questions. He had no idea *how* he became invisible, he said, and it wasn't actually a great treat being that way, since he often got bumped into, and had to keep reminding people he was there. After that, Teddy Talker thanked everyone for coming, and the show was over.

Back home, Arthur felt the evening had gone well.

'I got lots of applause,' he said. 'But maybe it was mostly because of what Stanley did. I shouldn't be too proud, I guess.'

'Poise and good humour contribute greatly to a performer's success,' said Mrs Lambchop. 'You did well on both those counts. Return Henry in the morning, dear. Time now for bed.'

The Bank Robbers

Mr Lambchop and Stanley and Arthur were watching the evening news on TV.

'. . . more dreadful scandal and violence tomorrow,' said the newscaster, ending a report on national affairs. 'Here in our fair city, another bank was robbed today, the third this month. The unusual robbers –'

'Enough of crime!' Bustling in, Mrs Lambchop switched off the TV. 'Come to dinner!'

Stanley supposed he would never know how the robbers were unusual. But the next afternoon, while strolling with Mr Lambchop, he found out. On the way home they passed a bank.

'I must cash a cheque, but it is very crowded in there,' said Mr Lambchop. 'Wait here, Stanley.'

Stanley waited.

Suddenly cries rose from within the bank. 'Lady bank robbers! Just like they said on TV! I laughed when I heard it! . . . Me too!'

Two women in dresses and fancy hats, one stout and the other very tall, ran out of the bank, each with a moneybag in one hand and a pistol in the other.

'Stay in there!' the stout woman called back into the bank, her voice high and scratchy. 'Don't anyone run out! Or else . . . Bang! Bang!'

'Right!' shouted the tall woman, also in an odd, high voice. 'Just because we are females doesn't mean we can't shoot!'

Being invisible won't protect me if bullets go flying about! Stanley thought. He looked for a place to hide.

An empty Yum-Yum Ice-Cream van was parked close by, and he jumped into it. His balloon still floated outside the van, its string caught in the door, but he did not dare to rescue it. Scrunching down behind cardboard barrels marked 'Yum Chocolate', 'Strawberry Yum', and 'Yum Crunch', he peeked out.

An alarm was ringing inside the bank,

and now shouts rose again. 'Ha! Now you're in trouble! The police will come! . . . Put that money back where you found it, ladies!'

Then Stanley saw that the two robber women were running towards him, carrying their money bags. They were stopping! They were getting into the Yum–Yum van!

Scrunching down again, he held his breath.

The robbers were in the van, close by where he hid. 'Hurry up!' said the stout woman, in a surprisingly deep voice. 'These shoes are killing me!'

The tall woman opened the 'Yum Crunch' barrel, and Stanley saw that it was empty. Then both robbers poured packets of money from their bags into the barrel, and put the lid back on again.

Stanley could hardly believe what he saw next!

The robbers threw aside their fancy hats, and tugged off wigs! And now they were undressing, pulling their dresses over their heads!

They were *men*, Stanley realised, not women! Yes! Underneath the dresses they wore white ice-cream-man pants, with the legs rolled up, and white Yum Yum shirts!

'Whew! What a relief, Howard!' The stout robber kicked off his women's shoes, and put on white sneakers.

'They'll never catch us now, Ralph!' said the tall one.

The robbers unrolled their trouser legs and threw their female clothing into

another empty barrel, the one marked 'Yum Chocolate'. Then they jumped into the front seats, the tall man driving, and the van sped off.

Behind the barrels, Stanley held his breath again. The pair was too clever to be caught! They were sure to get away! No one would suspect two Yum-Yum men of being lady – But the van was slowing! It was stopping.

Stanley peeked out again.

A police car blocked the road, and two policemen stood beside it, inspecting cars as they passed by. In a moment, they were at the Yum-Yum van.

'A bank got robbed,' the first policeman told the driver. 'By two women. You ice-cream fellows seen any suspicious looking females?'

'My!' The tall man shook his head. 'More and more these days, women filling roles once played by men. Bless 'em I say!'

Beside him, the stout man said hastily, 'But bank robbing, Howard, that's *wrong*.'

The second policeman looked into the back of the van. 'Just ice-cream here,' he told his partner.

The trickery is working! Stanley thought. How can I –? An idea came to him. Reaching out, he flipped the lid off the 'Yum Chocolate' barrel.

'Loose lid,' said the second policeman. 'Better tighten – Hey! This barrel is full of female clothes!'

'Oh!' The tall robber made a sad face. 'For the needy,' he said. 'They were my late mother's.'

Stanley flipped the the lid off the 'Yum

Crunch' barrel, and the packets of money were plain to see!

'Your mother was a mighty rich woman!' shouted the first policeman, drawing his pistol. 'Hands up, you two!'

As the robbers were being handcuffed, another police car drove up. Mr Lambchop jumped out of it.

'That balloon, on that van!' he shouted. 'We've been following it! Stanley? . . . Are you in there?'

'Yes!' Stanley called back. 'I'm fine. The bank robbers are caught! They weren't

ladies at all, just dressed that way!'

The handcuffed robbers were dreadfully confused. 'Who's yelling in our van? . . . Who stuck a balloon in the door? . . . Have we gone crazy?' they said.

'It's my son, Stanley,' said Mr Lambchop. 'He is invisible, unfortunately. Thank goodness he was not hurt!'

'That must be the same invisible boy they had on TV!' said the first policeman.

'An invisible boy?' The tall robber groaned. 'After all my careful planning!'

The stout robber shrugged. 'You can't think of *everything*, Howard. Don't blame yourself.'

The robbers were driven off to jail, and Stanley went home with Mr Lambchop in a cab.

Stanley had been *far* too brave, Mrs

Lambchop said when she heard what he had done. Really! Flipping those ice-cream lids! Arthur said he'd have flipped them too, if he'd thought of it.

Chapter Seven

Arthur's Storm

Mr and Mrs Lambchop had said goodnight. For a moment the brothers lay silent in their beds.

Then Arthur yawned. 'Goodnight, Stanley. Pleasant dreams.'

'Pleasant dreams? Hah!'

'Hah?'

'Those robbers today, they had *guns*!' said Stanley. 'I could have got shot by accident, and nobody would even know.'

'I never thought of that.' Arthur sat up. 'Are you mad at me?'

'I guess not. But . . .' Stanley sighed. 'The thing is, I don't want to go on being invisible. I was really scared today, and I hate carrying that balloon, but when I don't people bump into me. And I can't see myself in the mirror, so I don't even remember how I look! It's like when I was flat. It was all right for a while, but then people laughed at me.'

'That's why I blew you round again,' Arthur said proudly. 'Everyone said how smart I was.'

'If you're so smart, get me out of *this* fix!' There was a little tremble in Stanley's voice.

Arthur went to sit on the edge of his

brother's bed. Feeling for a foot beneath the covers, he patted it. 'I'm really sorry for you,' he said. 'I wish —'

There was a knock at the door, and Mr and Mrs Lambchop came in. 'Talking, you two? You ought to be asleep,' they said.

Arthur explained about Stanley's unhappiness.

'There's more,' Stanley said. 'Twice my friends had parties, and didn't invite me. They forget me sometimes even if I *do* keep waving that balloon!'

'Poor dear!' Mrs Lambchop said. '"Out of sight, out of mind," as the saying goes.' She went to put her arms around Stanley, but he had just sat up in bed, and she missed him. She found him and gave him a hug.

'This is awful!' Arthur said. 'We have to

do something!'

Mr Lambchop shook his head. 'Doctor Dan knew of no cure for Stanley's condition. And little about its cause, except for a possible connection between bad weather and fruit.'

'Then I'll always be like this.' Stanley's voice trembled again. 'I'll get older and bigger, but no one will ever see.'

Arthur was thinking. 'Stanley did eat fruit. And there *was* a storm. Maybe – Wait!'

He explained his idea.

Mr and Mrs Lambchop looked at each other, then at where they supposed Stanley to be, and at each other again.

'I'm not afraid,' said Stanley. 'Let's *try*!'

Mr Lambchop nodded. 'I see no harm in it.'

'Nor I,' said Mrs Lambchop. 'Very well,

Arthur! Let us gather what your plan requires!'

'Everyone ready?' said Arthur. 'It has to be just the way it was the night Stanley got invisible.'

'I'm wearing the same blue-and-white stripey pyjamas,' said Stanley. 'And I have an apple. And a box of raisins.'

'We can't make a real storm,' Arthur said. 'But maybe this will work.'

He stepped into the bathroom and ran the water in the basin and shower. 'There's rain,' he said, returning. 'I'll be wind.'

Mrs Lambchop held up a wooden spoon and a large frying-pan from her kitchen. 'Thunder ready,' she said.

Mr Lambchop showed the powerful torch he had fetched from his tool kit.

'Lightning ready.'

Stanley raised his apple. 'Now?'

'Go stand by the window,' said Arthur. 'Now let me think. Hmmm . . . It was dark.' He put out the light. 'Go on, eat. *Whooosh*!' he added, being wind.

Stanley began to eat the apple.

Water pattered down in the bathroom, into the basin and from the shower into the bathtub.

'*Whooosh . . . whooosh*!' said Arthur, and Mrs Lambchop struck her frying-pan with the wooden spoon. The *crash*! was much like thunder.

'Lightning, please,' Arthur said.

Mr Lambchop aimed his torch and flicked it on and off while Stanley finished the apple.

'Now the raisins,' said Arthur. 'One at a time.

Whooosh!'

Stanley opened the little box and ate a raisin.

Still *whooshing*, Arthur conducted as if an orchestra sat before him. His left hand signalled Mrs Lambchop to strike the frying pan, the right one Mr Lambchop to flash the light. Nods told Stanley when to eat a raisin.

Patter . . . splash . . . went the water in the bathroom. *Whooosh!* went Arthur. *Crash!* went the frying-pan. *Flash! . . . flash!* went the light.

'If anyone should see us now,' Mrs Lambchop said softly, 'I should be hard put to explain.'

Stanley looked down at himself. 'It's no use,' he said. 'I'm still invisible.'

'Twist around!' said Arthur. 'Maybe the

noise and light have to hit you just a certain way!'

Twisting, Stanley ate three more raisins. The light flickered over him. He heard the water splashing, Arthur *whoooshing*, the pounding of the frying-pan by the spoon. How hard they were trying, he thought. How much he loved them all!

But he was still invisible.

'There's only one raisin left,' he said. 'It's no use.'

'Poor Stanley!' cried Mrs Lambchop.

Arthur could not bear the thought of never seeing his brother again. 'Do the last raisin, Stanley,' he said. 'Do it!'

Stanley ate the raisin, and did one more twist. Mrs Lambchop tapped her frying-pan and Mr Lambchop flashed his light. Arthur gave a last *whooosh*!

Nothing happened.

'At least I'm not hungry,' Stanley said bravely. 'But –' He put a hand to his cheek. 'I feel . . . Sort of tingly.'

'Stanley!' said Mr Lambchop. 'Are you touching your cheek? I see your hand, I think!'

'And your pyjamas!' shouted Arthur, switching on the light.

A sort of outline of Stanley Lambchop, with hazy stripes running up and down it, had appeared by the window. Through the stripes, they could see the house next door.

Suddenly, the outline filled in. There stood Stanley in his striped pyjamas, just as they remembered him!

'I can see my feet!' Stanley shouted. 'It's *me*!'

'"*I*," dear, not "me!",' said Mrs Lambchop before she could catch herself, then ran to hold him tight.

Mr Lambchop shook hands with Arthur, and then they all went into the bathroom to watch Stanley look at himself in the mirror. It hadn't mattered when he was invisible, Mrs Lambchop said, but he was greatly in need of a haircut now.

She made hot chocolate to celebrate the occasion, and Arthur's cleverness was acknowledged by all.

'But false storms cannot be relied upon,' Mr Lambchop said. 'We must think twice before eating fruit during bad weather. Especially by a window.'

Then the brothers were tucked into bed again. 'Goodnight,' said Mr and Mrs Lambchop, putting out the light.

'Goodnight,' said Stanley and Arthur.

Stanley got up and went to have another look in the bathroom mirror. 'Thank you, Arthur,' he said, returning. 'You saved me from being flat, and now you've saved me again.'

'Oh, well . . .' Arthur yawned. 'Stanley?

Try to stay, you know, *regular* for a while.'

'I will,' said Stanley.

Soon they were both asleep.

FLAT STANLEY

Stanley in Space

'Will you meet with us?
Does anyone hear?'
From the great farness of space,
from farther than any planet or
star that has ever been mentioned
in books, the questions came.
Again and again.
'Will you meet with us?
Does anyone hear?'

The Call

It was Saturday morning, and Mr and Mrs Lambchop were putting up wallpaper in the kitchen.

'Isn't this nice, George?' said Mrs Lambchop, stirring paste. 'No excitement. A perfectly *usual* day.'

Mr Lambchop knew just what she meant. Excitement was often troublesome. The flatness of their son

Stanley, for example, after his big bulletin board settled on him overnight. Exciting, but worrying too, till Stanley got round again. And that genie visiting, granting wishes. Oh, very exciting! But all the wishes had to be *unwished* before the genie returned to the lamp from which he sprung.

'Yes, dear.' Mr Lambchop smoothed down wallpaper. 'Ordinary. The very best sort of day.'

In the living-room, Stanley Lambchop and his younger brother Arthur were watching a Tom Toad cartoon on TV. The sporty Toad was water-skiing and fell off, making a great splash. Arthur laughed so hard he didn't hear the telephone, but Stanley answered it.

'Lambchop residence?' said the caller.

'The President of the United States speaking. Who's this?'

Stanley smiled. 'The King of France.'

'They don't have kings in France. Not any more.'

'Excuse me, but I'm too busy for jokes.' Stanley kept his eyes on the TV. 'My brother and I are watching the Tom Toad Show.'

'Well, you *keep* watching, young fellow!' The caller hung up, just as Mr and Mrs Lambchop came in to watch the rest of the show.

'Hey, guess what?' Stanley said.

'Hay is for horses,' said Mrs Lambchop, mindful always of careful speech. 'Who called, dear?'

Stanley laughed. 'The President of the United States!'

Arthur laughed too. 'Stanley said *he* was the King of France!'

Tom Toad vanished suddenly from the TV screen, and an American flag appeared. 'We bring you a special message from the White House in Washington, DC,' said the deep voice of an announcer. 'Ladies and gentlemen, the President of the United States!'

The screen showed the President, looking very serious, behind his desk.

'My fellow Americans,' the President said. 'I am sorry to interrupt this programme, but someone out there doesn't realise that I am a very busy man who can't waste time joking on the telephone. I hope the particular person I am talking to – and I do *not* mean the King of France! – will remember that. Thank you. Now here's The Toad Show again.'

Tom Toad, still water-skiing, came back on the TV.

'Stanley!' exclaimed Mrs Lambchop. 'The King of France indeed!'

'Gosh!' Arthur said. 'Will Stanley get put in jail?'

'There is no law against being a

telephone smarty,' Mr Lambchop said. 'Perhaps there should be.'

The telephone rang, and he answered it. 'George Lambchop here.'

'Good!' It was the President. 'I've been trying to get hold of you!'

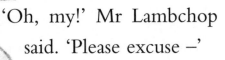

'Oh, my!' Mr Lambchop said. 'Please excuse –'

'Hold on. You're the fellow has the boy who was flat once, got his picture in the newspaper?'

'My son Stanley, Mr President,' Mr Lambchop said, to let the others know who was calling.

'I had to be sure,' said the President. 'We have to get together, Lambchop! I'll send my private plane right now, fetch you all here to Washington, DC.'

Mr Lambchop gasped. 'Private plane? Washington? *All* of us?'

'The whole family.' The President chuckled. 'Including the King of France.'

Washington

At the White House, in his famous Oval Office, the President shook hands with all the Lambchops.

'Thanks for coming.' He chuckled. 'Bet you never thought when you woke up this morning that you'd get to meet me.'

'Indeed not,' Mr Lambchop said. 'This is quite a surprise.'

'Well, here's another one,' said the President. 'The reason I asked you to come.'

He sat down behind his desk, serious now. 'Tyrra! Never heard of it, right?'

The Lambchops all shook their heads.

'*Nobody* ever heard of it. It's a planet, up there somewhere. They sent a message, the first ever from outer space!'

The Lambchops were greatly

interested. 'Imagine!' Mrs Lambchop exclaimed. 'What did it say?'

'Very friendly tone,' the President said. 'Peaceful, just checking around. Asked us to visit. Now, my plan –'

A side door of the Oval Office had opened suddenly to reveal a nicely-dressed lady wearing a crown. Mrs Lambchop recognised her at once as the Queen of England.

'About the banquet, also the −' the Queen began, and saw that the President was busy. 'Ooops! We beg your pardon.' She closed the door.

'This place is a *madhouse*,' the President said. 'Visitors, fancy dinners, no end to it. Now, where −? Ah, yes! The *Star Scout*!'

He leaned forward.

'That's our new top-secret spaceship, just ready now! Send somebody up in the *Star Scout*, I thought, to meet with these Tyrrans. But who? Wouldn't look peaceful to send soldiers, or even scientists. Then I thought: What could be more peaceful than just an ordinary American boy?'

The President smiled. 'Why not Stanley Lambchop?'

'Stanley?' Mrs Lambchop gasped. 'In a

spaceship? To meet with an alien race?'

'Oh, boy!' said Stanley. 'I would love to go!'

'Me, too,' said Arthur. 'It's not fair if –'

'Arthur!' Mr Lambchop drew in a deep breath. 'Mr President, why *Stanley*?'

'It has to be someone that's already had adventure experience,' the President said. 'Well, my Secret Service showed me a newspaper story about when Stanley was flat and caught two robbers. Robbers! That's adventure!'

'I've had them too!' Arthur said. 'A genie taught me to fly, and we had a Liophant, and –'

'A *what*?'

'A Liophant,' Arthur said. 'Half lion, half elephant. They're nice.'

15

'Is that right? The Secret Service never –'

'Mr President?' Mrs Lambchop did not like to interrupt, but her concern was great.

'Mr President?' she said. 'This *mission*: is it safe?'

'My goodness, of course it's safe!' the President said. 'We have taken great care, Mrs Lambchop. The *Star Scout* has all the latest scientific equipment. And it has been very carefully tested. First, we tried it on automatic pilot, with no passengers. It worked perfectly! Even then, ma'am, we were not satisfied. We sent the *Star Scout* up again, this time with our cleverest trained bird aboard. But hear for yourself.' The President spoke into a little box on his desk. 'Send

16

in Dr Schwartz, please.'

A bearded man entered, wearing a white coat and carrying a birdcage with a cloth over it. Bowing, he removed the cloth to reveal a large, brightly-coloured parrot.

'Thank you, Herman,' the President said. 'Dr Schwartz is our top space

scientist,' he told the Lambchops, 'and this is Polly, the bird I spoke of. Polly, tell the folks here about your adventure into space.'

'Piece of cake,' said the parrot. 'Terrific! Loved every minute of it!'

'Thank you, Herman,' the President said, and Dr Schwartz carried Polly away.

'That was very reassuring, but it is out of the question for Stanley to go alone,' Mrs Lambchop said. 'However, we *were* planning a family vacation. Would it be possible, Mr President, for us all to go?'

'Well, if you didn't mind the crowding,' the President said. 'And skimped on baggage.'

'Actually, we had in mind the seaside,' Mr Lambchop said. 'Or a tennis camp. But −'

The Queen of England looked in again. 'May we ask if –'

'Just a *minute*, for heaven's sake!' said the President.

'We shall return anon.' Looking peeved, the Queen went away.

Mr Lambchop had decided. 'Mr President, the seaside will keep. We will go to Tyrra, sir.'

'Wonderful!' The President jumped up. 'To the stars, Lambchops! Some training at the Space Centre, and you're on your way!'

Chapter Three

Taking Off

'Ten!' said the voice of Mission Control.

The count-down had begun. When it reached 'Zero' Chief Pilot Stanley Lambchop would press the 'Start' button, and the *Star Scout* would blast off for Tyrra.

'Nine!'

Strapped into their seats, the Lambchops held their breaths, each thinking very different thoughts.

Stanley was wondering if the Tyrrans would mind that Earth had sent just an ordinary family. Suppose they were big stuck-ups and expected a general or a TV star, or even the President? Suppose –

'Eight!' said Control, and Stanley fixed his eyes on the panel before him.

Mr Lambchop was thinking that serving one's country was noble, but this was a bit much. How did these things happen? Off to an unknown planet, the entire family! Other families didn't have a son become flat. Other families didn't find genies in the house. Other – Oh, well! Mr Lambchop sighed.

'Seven!' said Control.

Mrs Lambchop thought that Mr

Lambchop seemed fretful. But why, now the *Star Scout* looked so *nice*? Thanks to her, in fact. 'They may call it a spaceship,' she had said when she first saw it, 'but where's the *space*? Just one room! And all grey . . .? Drab, I say!' Much of the training at the Space Centre, however, was physical, and Mrs Lambchop, who jogged and exercised regularly, quickly passed the tests required. In the days that followed, while the others were being made fit, she used her free time to make the *Star Scout* more like home. Only so much weight was permitted, but she managed a bathroom scale for the shower alcove and a plastic curtain, pretty shades for the portholes, a Venetian blind for the Magnifying Exploration Window, and posters of Mexico and France.

'Six! . . . Five! . . . Four! . . . Three! . . .'

Mrs Lambchop made sure her purse
was snug beneath her seat.

Arthur, by nature lazy, was thinking
that he was glad to be done with all
the jogging, jumping, climbing ladders,
and scaling walls. When he was super-
strong, thanks to the genie, it would
have been easy. But for just plain
Arthur Lambchop, he thought, it
was tiring.

'Two!' said Control. 'Good
luck, everybody! One!'

'Pay attention, dear,'
Mrs Lambchop told
Stanley.

'Zero!' said
Control,

and Stanley pressed the 'Start' button.

Whrooom! Rockets roaring, the *Star Scout* rose from its launching pad.

Whroooooom! *Whroooooom!* Gaining speed, it soared higher and higher, carrying the Lambchops towards the farness where Tyrra lay.

In Space

'I'll just flip this omelette,' said Mrs Lambchop, making breakfast in the *Star Scout*, 'and then – Oh, dear!' The omelette hovered like a Frisbee in the air above her.

Mostly, however, after weeks in space, the Lambchops remembered that gravity, the force that held things down, did not exist beyond Earth's atmosphere.

Mr Lambchop often read now with his hands clasped behind his head, allowing his book to float before him, and Stanley and Arthur greatly enjoyed pushing from their chairs to drift like feathers across the room.

Raising her pan, Mrs Lambchop brought down the omelette. 'After breakfast, what?' she said. 'A game of *Monopoly*?'

'Please, not again.' Arthur sighed. 'If I'd known this adventure would be so boring, I'd never have come.'

'The worst part,' Stanley said, 'is not knowing how long it will last.'

'The beginning wasn't boring,' Arthur said as they began their breakfast. 'The beginning was fun.'

The first days had in fact been tremendously exciting. They had spent many hours at the *Star Scout*'s Magnifying Window, watching the bright globe of Earth grow steadily smaller, until it seemed at last only a pale marble in the black of space. And there had been many special sights to see: the starry beauty of the Milky Way, the planets – red Mars, giant Jupiter, cloudy Venus, Saturn with its shining rings.

The third evening they appeared on TV news broadcasts on Earth. Word of their voyage had been released to the press, and all over the world people were eager to learn how this extraordinary adventure was proceeding. Standing before the spaceship's camera, the Lambchops said they felt fine, looked forward to meeting the Tyrrans, and would report nightly while they remained in TV range.

The fourth evening they floated before the camera, demonstrating weightlessness. This was greatly appreciated on Earth, and they floated again the following day.

By the sixth evening, however, they were hard-pressed to liven their appearances. Mr Lambchop recited a

baseball poem, 'Casey At The Bat'. Stanley juggled tennis balls, but the Earth audience, knowing now about weightlessness, saw the balls float when he tossed them up. Arthur did imitations of a rooster, a dog, and a man stuck in a phone booth. After this, while Mrs Lambchop was singing her college song, he went behind the plastic curtain to undress for a shower and accidentally pulled the curtain down. He was mortified, and she tried later to comfort him.

'We will be remembered, Arthur, for our time in space,' she said. 'Nobody will care about a curtain.'

'I will be remembered *forever*,' Arthur said. 'A hundred million people saw me in my underwear.'

The next day was Stanley's birthday, and just after dinner the screen lit up. There was the President in his shirtsleeves, behind his desk in Washington, DC.

'Well, here I am working late again,' the President said. 'It's a tough job, believe me. Happy birthday, Stanley Lambchop! I've arranged a surprise. First, your friends from school.'

There was silence for a moment, broken only by the clearing of throats, and then, from all the millions of miles away, came the voices of Stanley's classmates singing, 'Happy Birthday, dear Stanley! Happy Birthday to you!'

Stanley was tremendously pleased. 'Thanks, everybody!' he said. 'You too, Mr President.'

'That was just the USA part,' said the President. 'Ready over there in London, Queen?'

'We are indeed,' the Queen's voice said cheerfully. 'And now, Master Lambchop, our famous Westminster Boys' Choir!'

From England, the beautiful voices of the famous choir sang 'Happy Birthday,

Stanley!' all over again, and then other children sang it from Germany, Spain, and France.

All this attention to Stanley made Arthur jealous, and when the President said, 'By the way, Arthur, you entertained us wonderfully the other night,' he was sure this was a tease about his appearance in underwear. But he was wrong.

'Those imitations!' the President said. 'Especially the fellow in the phone booth. Darn good!'

'Indeed!' the Queen added from England. 'We were greatly amused.'

'Oh, thank you!' said Arthur, cheered. 'I –'

The screen had gone blank.

They had travelled too far. There would be no more voices from Earth, no voices but their own until they heard what the Tyrrans had to say.

'Suppose the Tyrrans have forgotten we're coming?' Stanley said. 'We might just sail around in space *forever.*'

They had finished the breakfast omelette, and were now setting out the *Monopoly* board because there was nothing more interesting to do.

'They don't even know our names,' Arthur said. 'What will they call us?'

'Earth people!' said a deep voice.

'Very probably,' said Mr Lambchop. '"Earth people" seems – Who said that?'

'Not me,' said both Stanley and Arthur.

'Not *I*,' said Mrs Lambchop, correcting. 'But who –'

'Earth people!' The voice, louder now, came from the *Star Scout*'s radio. 'Greetings from the great planet Tyrra and its mighty people! Do you hear?'

'Oh, my!' Mr Lambchop turned up the volume. 'It's them!'

'*They*,' said Mrs Lambchop.

'For heaven's sake, Harriet!' Mr Lambchop said, and spoke loudly into the microphone. 'Hello, Tyrra. Earth people here. Party of four. Peace-loving family.'

'Peace-loving?' said the voice. 'Good! So is mighty Tyrra! Where are you, Earth people?'

Stanley checked his star maps. 'We're just where the tail of Ralph's Comet meets star number three million and forty-seven. Now what?'

'Right,' said the Tyrran voice. 'Keep going till you pass a star formation that looks like a foot. You can't miss it. Then, just past a lopsided little white moon, start down. You'll see a pointy mountain, then a big field. Land there. See you soon, Earth people!'

'You bet!' Mr Lambchop said, and turned to his family. 'The first contact with another planet!

We are making history!'

They passed the foot-shaped star formation, then the lopsided moon, and Stanley piloted the *Star Scout* down.

The darkness of space vanished as it descended, and at last the Lambchops saw clearly the planet it had taken so long to reach.

Tyrra was smallish as planets go, but nicely round and quite pretty, all in shades of brown with markings not unlike the oceans and continents of Earth. A pointy mountain came into sight, and beyond it a big field.

'There!' Stanley pressed the 'Landing' button.

Whrooom! went the *Star Scout's* rockets. The spaceship hovered, then touched down.

Peering out, the Lambchops saw only a brown field, with tan trees at the far side and brownish hills beyond.

'Curious,' said Mr Lambchop. 'Where are —'

Suddenly a message came, but not the sort they expected.

'Surrender, Earth people!' said the radio. 'Your spaceship is trapped by our unbreakable trapping cable! You are prisoners of Tyrra! Surrender!'

The Tyrrans

Unbreakable trapping cable? Prisoners? Surrender? The Lambchops could scarcely believe their ears.

'I don't call *that* peaceful,' said Mrs Lambchop. 'Our President has been misled.'

'I wish we had gone to the seaside.' Mr Lambchop shook his head. 'But *how* are we trapped? I don't –' He pointed to the

Magnifying Window. 'What's that?'

A thin blue line, like a thread, had been passed over the *Star Scout*. Stanley switched on the wiper above the big window and the first flick of its blade parted the blue line.

'Drat!' said the radio.

Other voices rose, startled, and then the deep voice spoke again. 'Earth people! We're sending a messenger! A regular, ordinary Tyrran, just to show what we're like.'

For long moments, the Lambchops kept their eyes on the tan trees across the field.

'There!' Arthur said suddenly. 'Coming toward – Oh! Oh, my . . .' His voice trailed away.

The Tyrran messenger came slowly

forward to stand before the big window, a muscular, scowling young man with a curling moustache, wearing shorts and carrying a club.

The moustache was very large. The messenger was not.

'That man,' Mrs Lambchop said slowly, 'is only three inches tall.'

'At most,' Mr Lambchop said. 'It is a magnifying window.'

The Tyrran seemed to be calling something. Arthur opened the door a crack, and the words came clearly now. '– afraid to let us see you, Earth people? Because I'm so enormous? Hah! *All* Tyrrans are this big!'

Flinging the door wide, Arthur showed himself. 'Well, I'm a *small* Earth person!' he shouted. 'The rest are even bigger than me!'

'*I*, not me,' Mrs Lambchop said. 'And don't tease, Arth– Oh! He's fainted!'

Wetting her handkerchief with cold water, she jumped down from the *Star Scout* and ran to dab the Tyrran's tiny brow.

Cries rose again from the spaceship's radio. 'A giant killed Ik! . . . There's another, even bigger! . . . Oh, gross! . . . Look! Ik's all right!'

The Tyrran, by grasping Mrs Lambchop's handkerchief, had indeed pulled himself up. Furious, he swung his club, but managed only to tap the top of her shoe. 'Ouch! Scat!' she said, and he darted back across the field.

'Oh, my!' said the radio. 'Never mind about surrendering, Earth people! A truce committee is on the way!'

At first they saw only a tiny flag, fluttering like a white butterfly far across the brown field, but at last the Tyrran committee drew close, and the Lambchops, waiting now outside the *Star Scout*, could make each little person out.

The flag was carried by the scowling young man with the moustache and the club. The other members of the committee, a bit smaller even than he, were a red-faced man wearing a uniform with medals across the chest, a stout lady in a yellow dress and a hat with flowers on it, and two older men in blue suits, one with wavy white hair, the other thin and bald.

The committee halted, staring bravely up.

'I am General Ap!' shouted the uniformed man. 'Commander of all Tyrran forces!'

Stanley stepped forward. 'Chief Pilot Stanley Lambchop,' he said. 'From Earth. These are my parents, Mr and Mrs George Lambchop. And my brother Arthur.'

'President Ot of Tyrra, and Mrs Ot,' said General Ap, indicating the wavy-haired man and the lady. 'The bald chap is Dr Ep, our Chief Scientist. The grouchy one with the flag is my aide, Captain Ik.'

No one seemed sure what to say next. A few polite remarks were exchanged – 'Nice meeting you, Earth people!' . . . 'Such a pretty planet, Tyrra!' . . . 'Thank you. Were you very long in space?' – and Mr Lambchop realised suddenly that the Tyrrans were uncomfortable talking almost straight up. He got down on his knees, the other Lambchops following his example, and the Tyrrans at once lowered their heads in relief.

'Right!' said General Ap. 'All reasonable people here! A truce, eh?'

'I'm for war, frankly,' growled Captain Ik, but Stanley pretended not to hear. 'A truce? Good idea,' he said. 'We come in peace.'

Mrs Ot sniffed. 'Not very peaceful, frightening poor Captain Ik.' She pointed at Arthur. 'That giant shouted at him!'

'My son is not a giant,' Mrs Lambchop said. 'It's just that you Tyrrans are – how to put it? – unusually *petite.*'

'Ik's the biggest we've got, actually,' said General Ap. 'We hoped he'd scare you.'

President Ot raised his hand. 'No harm done! Come! TyrraVille, our capital, is but a stroll away.'

The Lambchops, equipped now with handy magnifying lenses from the *Star Scout*'s science kit, followed the committee.

TyrraVille lay just across the brown field, behind the tan trees, no larger than an Earth-size tennis court.

TyrraVille

'Gosh!' Stanley said. 'It makes me homesick, in a way.'

Except for its size, and the lack of greenness, the Tyrran capital was indeed much like a small village on Earth. A Main Street bustled with Tyrrans shopping and running errands; there were handsome school and public buildings, two churches with spires as

high as Mr Lambchop's waist, and side streets of pretty houses with lawns like neat brown postage stamps.

Captain Ik, still angry, marched on ahead, but the rest of the committee halted at the head of Main Street.

'We'll just show you *around*, eh?' said President Ot. 'Safer, I think.'

The Lambchops saw at once the risk of walking streets scarcely wider than their feet. Escorted by the committee, they circled the little capital, bending

often to make use of their magnifying lenses. Mrs Ot took care to indicate points of particular interest, among them Ux Field, a sports centre, Admiral Ux Square, Ux Park, and the Ux Science Centre Building. ('Mrs Ot's grandfather,' whispered General Ap. 'Very rich!')

The tour caused a great stir. Everywhere the tiny citizens of TyrraVille waved from windows and rooftops. At the Science Centre, the last stop, journalists took photographs, and the Lambchops were treated to Grape Fizzola, the Tyrran national drink, hundreds of bottles of which were emptied into four tubs to make Earth-size portions.

Refreshed by his Fizzola, Arthur took a little run and hurdled a large part of TyrraVille, landing in Ux Square. 'Arthur!' Mrs Lambchop scolded, and he hurdled back.

'Aren't kids the dickens?' said a Tyrran mother, looking on. 'Mine – Stop *tugging*, Herbert!' These last words seemed addressed to the ground beside her. 'My youngest,' she explained.

Stanley squinted. 'I can hardly – He's just a *dot*.'

'Dot yourself!' said an angry voice. 'Big-a-rooney! *You're* the funny-looking one!'

'Herbert!' his mother said. 'It is rude to make fun of people for their shape or size!'

'As I said myself, often, when Stanley was flat!' Mrs Lambchop exclaimed. 'If only –'

'Surrender, Earth people!'

The cry had come from Captain Ik, who appeared now from behind the Science Centre, staggering beneath the weight of a box-like machine almost as big as he was, with a tube sticking out of it.

'Surrender!' he shouted. 'You cannot resist our Magno-Titanic Paralyser Ray! Tyrra will yet be saved!'

'There's a truce, Ik!' barked General Ap. 'You can't –'

'Yes, I can! First – Ooops!' Captain Ik's

knees had buckled, but he recovered himself. 'First I'll paralyse the one who scared me back there in the field!'

Yellow light flickered up at Arthur from the Magno-Titanic Paralyser.

'Yikes!' said Arthur, as shrieks rose from the crowd.

But it was not on Arthur that the Magno-Titanic beam landed. Stanley had sprung forward to protect his brother, and the light shone now on his chest and shoulders. Mrs Lambchop almost fainted.

Suddenly her fright was gone.

Stanley was smiling. The yellow rays still flickering upon him, he rolled his head and wiggled his hands to show that he was fine. 'It's nice, actually,' he said. 'Like a massage.'

The crowd hooted. 'It only works on people Tyrran size!' someone called. 'You're a ninny, Ik!' Then Captain Ik was marched off by a Tyrran policeman, and the crowd, still laughing, drifted away.

Mrs Lambchop spoke sternly to the committee. '"Tyrra will yet be saved?" What did Captain Ik mean? And why, pray tell, did he attempt to paralyse my son?'

The Ots and General Ap exchanged glances. Dr Ep stared at the ground.

'Ah!' said President Ot. 'Well . . . The fact is, we're having a . . . a crisis, actually. Yes. And Ik, well, he, ah –'

'Oh, tell them!' Mrs Ot burst suddenly into tears. 'About the Super-Gro! Tell, for heaven's sake!'

Puzzled, the Lambchops stared at her. The sky had darkened, and now a light rain began to fall.

'Wettish, eh?' said General Ap. 'Can't offer shelter, I'm afraid. No place large enough.'

'The *Star Scout* will do nicely,' said Mrs Lambchop. 'Let us return to it for tea.'

President Ot's Story

'Tea *does* help. I am quite myself again.' Mrs Ot nodded to her husband. 'Go on, dear. Tell.'

Rain drummed faintly on the *Star Scout*, making even cosier the scene within. About the dining-table, the Lambchops occupied their usual places. The Tyrrans sat atop the table on thumbtacks pushed down to serve as stools, sipping from tiny cups Mrs Lambchop had fashioned from aluminium foil, and nibbling crumbs of her home-made ginger snaps.

Now, sighing, President Ot set down his cup.

'You will have observed, Lambchops,' he said, 'how greatly we have enjoyed these tasty refreshments. The fact is, Tyrra has for some time been totally without fresh food or water fit to drink. We live now only by what tins and bottles we had in store.'

Mrs Ot made a face. 'Pink meat spreads, and spinach. And that *dreadful* Fizzola.'

'A bit sweet, yes,' said General Ap. 'Gives one gas, too. But –'

'Never mind!' cried Mrs Ot.

President Ot continued. 'The cause

of our tragedy, Lambchops, was Super-Gro. An invention of Dr Ep's. Super-Gro, Ep promised, would double our crops, make them double size, double delicious as well. A great concept, he said.'

'We scientists,' said Dr Ep, 'dream larger than other men.'

'For three days, at the Science Centre,' President Ot went on, 'Ep brewed his Super-Gro. Great smelly vats of it, enough for the whole planet. But then . . . Oh, no Tyrran will ever forget that fourth day! I myself was strolling through Ux Park. How beautiful it was! The trees and grass so green, the sky –'

'Green?' said Arthur. 'But everything's *brown* here, not green!'

'A mishap,' murmured Dr Ep. 'With the Super-Gro.'

'Mishap?' barked General Ap. 'The stuff *exploded*, Ep! All over the place!'

'Well, nobody's perfect.' Dr Ep hung his head.

'All those huge vats, Lambchops!' President Ot continued. 'Boom! One after another! Shattered windows, blew the roof off the Science Centre! No one hurt, thank goodness, but great clouds of smoke, darkening the sky! And then – such dreadful luck – it began to rain. A *tremendous* rain, mixing with the smoke, falling all over Tyrra, into the rivers, on to every field and garden, every bit of greenery.'

Rising from his thumbtack, he paced back and forth across the table.

'When the rain stopped, there was no green. None. Just brown. Worse, Ep's tests proved that our water was undrinkable, and that nowhere on Tyrra would anything grow. I broadcast at once to the nation. "Do not despair," I said, "Tyrra will soon recover."'

'Oh, good!' Mr Lambchop said.

President Ot shook his head. 'I lied. I couldn't tell the truth, for fear of causing panic, you see. The tests showed that it would be a year at least before Tyrra was green again. And long before that we will have emptied our last tin, our last bottle of Fizzola.'

He sat down again, covering his face with his hands.

'So then we . . . We sent a message, into space. Lure some other planet's spaceship, we thought. Hold it for ransom, you see, make them send food and water. Oh, shameful! Underhanded. You will never forgive us, I know . . .'

His voice trailed away, and there was only the patter of the rain.

Close to tears, the Lambchops looked at each other, then at the little people on the table top. The Tyrrans seemed particularly tiny now, and brave, and nice.

'You poor dears!' Mrs Lambchop said. 'There was no need to *conquer* us. We would help you willingly, if we could.'

The Tyrrans seemed at first unable to believe their ears. Then, suddenly, their faces shone with joy.

'Bless you!' cried General Ap.

'Saved!' Mrs Ot clapped her hands. 'We are saved!'

'Saved . . .?' said Mrs Lambchop.

'Of course!' said President Ot. 'Don't you see? Earth's spaceships can bring food and water till – Oh! What's wrong?'

It was Arthur who explained.

'I'm very sorry,' he said. 'But there's just the *Star Scout*. Earth hasn't *got* any other spaceships. And it would take years to build them.'

The Tyrrans gasped. 'Years . . .?' said Dr Ep.

Stanley felt so sad he could hardly speak. 'And it's no use going for food in the *Star Scout*,' he said. 'By the time we returned from Earth, you'd all be –

Well, you know.'

'Dead,' said Mrs Ot.

In the *Star Scout*, a terrible silence fell. The facts were clear. The cupboards of Tyrra would soon be empty. And then all its tiny people would starve to death.

Stanley's Good Idea

The teapot was cold now, and a last cookie crumb lay unwanted on a plate. Gloom hung like a dark cloud within the *Star Scout*.

'It's not fair,' Arthur said for the third time. 'It just not.'

'Stop saying that,' Stanley told him. 'That's four times now.'

'Five,' said Dr Ep.

General Ap tried to be cheerful. 'Ah well . . . Still some tinned meat, eh? And plenty of Grape Fizzola. Much to be thankful for.'

'I will *never* be thankful for Grape Fizzola,' said Mrs Ot.

'It's just that . . .' Arthur sighed. 'I mean, Earth has so *much* food. Millions of people, and there's mostly still enough.'

The Tyrrans seemed amazed. 'Millions? You're joking?' said President Ot.

'Hah!' said General Ap. 'Dreadful crush, I should think. Millions?'

Mrs Lambchop smiled. 'With all our great nations, many millions. And still the numbers grow.'

'Well, here too.' President Ot shook his head. 'Youthful marriages, babies one after another. But *millions*? Our

76

population – there's just TyrraVille, of course – is six hundred and eighty-three.'

'Eighty-four,' said Mrs Ot. 'Mrs Ix had a baby last night.'

Now it was the Lambchops who were amazed.

'Just TyrraVille?' Arthur cried. 'But TyrraVille's your *capital*, you said!'

'Well, it would have to be, wouldn't it, dear?' said Mrs Ot.

Stanley shook his head. 'On the whole planet, only six hundred and eighty-four Tyrrans! Gosh, I'll bet – Wait!'

And idea had come to him. Stanley had had exciting ideas before, but none that excited him as this one did.

'Mrs Ot!' he shouted. 'How much do you weigh?'

'Stanley!' said Mrs Lambchop.

Mrs Ot was not offended. 'Actually, I've slimmed a bit. Though not, sadly, in the hips. I'm six ounces, young man. Why do you ask?'

The words rushed out of Stanley. 'Because if you're average only children would be even lighter, then all the Tyrrans put together would weigh – Let me figure this out!'

'Less than three hundred pounds,' said Mr Lambchop, who was good at maths. 'Though I don't see –' Then he did see. 'Oh! Good for you, Stanley!'

'The lad's bright, we know,' said General Ap. 'But what –'

'General!' said Mr Lambchop. 'Summon all Tyrrans here to the *Star Scout*! Fetch what remains of your tinned food and Grape Fizzola! Perhaps Earth can be your home till Tyrra is green again!'

The Weighing

From each little house on each little street, the Tyrrans came, every man, woman, and child, even Captain Ik with a guard from the jail. The rain had stopped, and the evening light shone gold on the brown field in which the tiny people stood assembled.

President Ot addressed them. 'Fellow Tyrrans! I must confess that your government has deceived you! The truth is: It will be at least a year before our fields and streams are fit again.'

Cries rose from the crowd. 'We were lied to! . . . Lordy, talk about bad news! . . . We'll starve! . . . Shoot the scientists!'

'Wait!' shouted President Ot. 'We are offered refuge on Earth, if the voyage is possible! Pay attention, please!'

Stepping forward, Mr Lambchop read aloud from the booklet that had come with the *Star Scout*.

'"Your spacecraft has been designed for safety as well as comfort. Use only as directed."' He raised his voice. '"Do not add weight by bringing souvenirs aboard *or by inviting friends to ride with you.*"'

Cries rose again. 'That did it! . . . We're not *souvenirs*! . . . He said no friends either, stupid! . . . We've had it, looks like!'

Mr Lambchop raised his hand. 'There is still hope! But you must all be weighed! Also the supplies you would require for the trip!'

The *Star Scout*'s bathroom scales, set down in the field, proved too high for the Tyrrans, and the weighing was briefly delayed until Arthur, using the *Monopoly* board, made a ramp by which they could easily mount.

General Ap barked orders. 'Right, then! Groups of twenty to twenty-five, families together! And don't jiggle!'

The Ots and six other families marched up on to the scales, beside which Mrs Lambchop stood with pad and pencil. 'Seven and one-quarter pounds!' she said, writing it down.

'Next!' shouted General Ap, but the Ot group was already starting down, and another marching up.

Group after group mounted the scales. There *was* jiggling, due to excited children, but Mrs Lambchop took care to wait until the needle was still. Within an hour the entire population of Tyrra had been weighed, along with its supplies of tinned food and Fizzola, and she added up.

'Tyrrans, two hundred and thirty-nine,'

she announced. 'Food and Fizzola, one hundred and forty. Total: Three hundred and seventy-nine pounds!'

'Are we saved? Or are we too fat?' came a cry.

'Too soon to tell!' Mr Lambchop called back. 'We must see how we can lighten our ship!'

A good start was made by discarding the *Star Scout*'s dining-table and one steel bunk, since Stanley and Arthur could easily share. Then out went Stanley's tennis balls, extra sweater, and his Chief Pilot zip jacket with the American flag; out went Arthur's knee socks, raincoat, and a plastic gorilla he had smuggled aboard. Mr and Mrs Lambchop added their extra clothing, lamps, kitchenware, the *Monopoly* game, and at last, the posters of Mexico and France.

The crowd stood hushed as the pile was weighed. Somewhere a baby cried, and its parents scolded it.

'Three hundred and seventy-seven pounds!' Mrs Lambchop announced. 'Oh, dear!' she whispered to President Ot. 'Two less than we need.'

'I see.' President Ot, after a moment's thought, climbed up on to the scale. 'Good news, Tyrrans!' he called. 'Almost all of us are saved!'

Cheers went up, and then someone shouted, 'What do you mean, *almost* all?'

'We weigh, as a nation, a bit too much,' President Ot explained. 'But only four, if largish, need stay behind. I shall be one. Will three more volunteer?'

Murmurs rose from the crowd. 'That's *my* kind of President! . . . Leave Ik behind! . . . How about you, Ralph? . . . Ask somebody else, darn you!'

The matter was quickly resolved. 'I

won't go without you, dear,' Mrs Ot told her husband, and Captain Ik, hoping to regain popularity, announced that he too would remain.

General Ap was the fourth volunteer. 'Just an old soldier, ma'am,' he told Mrs Lambchop. 'Lived a full life, time now to just fade away, to –'

'Hey! Wait!'

Arthur was pointing to the scales.

'We forgot *that*,' he said. 'We can leave the scales behind. Now nobody has to stay!'

Chapter Ten

Heading Home

'Mr and Mrs Ix, and the new baby?' said President Ot, beside his wife on a ledge above the Magnifying Window. 'Ah, yes, on the fridge!'

The people of Tyrra were being made as comfortable as possible in the various nooks and crannies of the *Star Scout*. Stanley and Arthur had cleared a cupboard where Tyrra High School students could study during the trip, and Mrs Lambchop had cut up sheets to make hundreds of little blankets, and put out bits of cotton for pillows. 'Makeshift, Mrs Ix,' she said now, settling the Ixes on the fridge. 'But *such* short notice. Back a bit from the edge, yes?'

'Short notice indeed,' said Mrs Ix. 'So many –'

'Not to worry.' Mrs Lambchop smiled proudly. 'My son, the Chief Pilot, will call ahead.'

From a nearby shelf, Captain Ik whispered an apology for attempting to paralyse Arthur. 'Between you and I, I didn't really think it would work,' he said.

'Between you and *me*,' said Mrs Lambchop. 'But thank you, Captain Ik.'

She turned to Stanley. 'We're all ready, dear!'

Stanley checked his controls. 'Let's go!'

'Tyrrans!' President Ot called for attention. 'Our national anthem!'

Everywhere in the *Star Scout*, Tyrrans rose, their right hands over their hearts. '*Hmmmm . . .*' hummed Mrs Ot, setting a key, and they began to sing.

> *Tyrra, the lovely! Tyrra, the free!*
> *Hear, dear planet, our promise to thee!*
> *Where e'er we may go, where e'er we*
> *may roam,*
> *We'll come back to Tyrra, Tyrra our home!*

The words echoed in the softly-lit cabin. Many Tyrrans were weeping, and the eyes of the Lambchops, as they took

their seats, glistened too.

> *Be it ever so humble, there's no planet*
> *so dear,*
> *We'll always love Tyrra, from far or*
> *from —*

Stanley pressed the 'Start' button, and – *Whroooom!* – the *Star Scout*'s rockets roared to life.

The singing stopped suddenly, and Mrs Ix cried out from the fridge. 'Oh, my! Is this thing safe?'

'Yes indeed,' Mrs Lambchop called back.

'Perhaps,' said Mrs Ix. 'But it is my belief that if Tyrrans were meant to fly, we'd have wings.'

Whroooom! Whroooom!

The *Star Scout* lifted now, gaining speed as it rose. Its mission was done. The strangers who had called from a distant planet were no longer strangers, but friends.

It was all very satisfactory, Stanley thought. The other Lambchops thought so too.

Earth Again

'. . . real pleasure to welcome you, Tyrrans,' said the President, almost done with his speech. 'I wish you a fine year on Earth!'

Before him on the White House lawn, with newspaper and TV reporters all about, sat the Lambchops and, in a tiny grandstand built especially for the occasion, the people of Tyrra.

The Tyrrans were now applauding politely, but they looked nervous, and Mrs Lambchop guessed why. That crowd at the Space Centre for the *Star Scout*'s landing, that drive through crowded streets into Washington, DC! Poor Tyrrans! Everywhere they looked, giant buildings, giant people. How could they feel comfortable here?

But a surprise was in store. Across the lawn, a great white sheet had been spread. Now, at the President's signal, workmen pulled the sheet away.

'Welcome,' said the President, 'to TyrraVille Two!'

Gasps rose from the Tyrrans, then shouts of joy.

Before them, on what had been the White House tennis court, lay an entire village of tiny houses, one for each Tyrran family, with shops and schools and churches, and a miniature railway serving all principal streets. Begun when Stanley called ahead from space, TyrraVille Two had been completed well before the *Star Scout*'s arrival, thanks to rush deliveries from leading toy stores in Washington and New York.

The excited Tyrrans ran from the grandstand to explore their new homes, and soon happy voices rose from every window and doorway of TyrraVille Two. 'Nice furniture! . . . Hooray! Fresh lemonade! No more Fizzola! . . . In the cupboards, see? Shirts, dresses, suits, shoes! . . . Underwear, even!'

The Ots, General Ap, Dr Ep, and Captain Ik came back to say goodbye, and the Lambchops knelt to touch fingertips in farewell. The TV men filmed this, and Arthur made everyone laugh, pretending to be paralysed by the touch of Captain Ik. Then the newsmen left, the Tyrrans returned to TyrraVille Two, and only the President remained with the Lambchops on the White House lawn.

'Well, back to work.' The President sighed. 'Goodbye, Lambchops. You're all heroes, you know. Saved the nation.'

'Not really,' Stanley said. 'They couldn't have conquered us.'

'Well, you know what I mean,' the President said. 'You folks care to stay for supper?'

'Thank you, no,' Mrs Lambchop said. 'It is quite late, and this has been an

exciting but very tiring day.'

It was bedtime when they got home. Stanley and Arthur had a light supper, with hot chocolate to help them sleep, after which Mr and Mrs Lambchop tucked them in and said goodnight.

The brothers lay quietly in the darkness for a moment. Then Arthur chuckled.

'The Magno-Titanic Paralyser *was* sort of scary,' he said. 'You were brave, Stanley, protecting me.'

'That's okay,' Stanley said. 'You're my brother, right?'

'I know . . .' Arthur was sleepy now. 'Stanley? When the Tyrrans go back, will their land and water be okay? Will they let us know?'

'I guess so.' Stanley was drowsy too. 'Goodnight, Arthur.'

'Goodnight,' said Arthur, and soon they were both asleep.

FLAT STANLEY

Stanley's Christmas Adventure

Prologue

She was the sort of little girl who liked to be *sure* of things, so she went all over Snow City, checking up.

The elves had done their work.

At the Post Office, Mail Elves had read the letters, making lists of who wanted what.

In the great workshops – the Doll Room, the Toy Plant, the Game Mill –

Gift Elves had filled the orders, taking care as to colour and size and style.

In the Wrap Shed the gifts lay ready, wrapped now in gay paper with holly and pine cones, sorted by country, by city or village, by road or lane or street.

The Wrap Elves teased her. 'Don't trust us, eh? . . . Snooping, we call this, Miss!'

'Pooh!' said the little girl. 'Well done, elves! Good work!'

But at home in Snow City Square, all was not well.

'Don't slam the door, dear,' said her mother weeping. 'Your father's having his nap.'

'Mother! What's wrong?'

'He won't go this year, he says!' the mother sobbed. 'He's been so cross lately, but I never –'

'*Why*? *Why* won't he go?'

'They've lost faith, don't care any more, he says! Surely not *everyone*, I said. Think of your favourite letter, the one by your desk! He just growled at me!'

'Pooh!' said the girl. 'It's not fair! Really! I mean, everything's *ready*! Why –'

'Not now, dear,' said the mother. 'It's been a dreadful day.'

In the little office at the back of the house, the girl studied the letter her mother had mentioned, framed with others on a wall:

I am a regular boy, except that I got flat, the letter said. *From an accident. I was going to ask for new clothes, but my mother already bought them. She had to, because of the flatness. So I'm just writing to say don't*

bother about me. Have a nice holiday. My
father says be careful driving, there are lots
of bad drivers this time of year.

The girl thought for a moment, and an
idea came to her. 'Hmmmm . . . Well,
why *not*?' she said.

She looked again at the letter.

The name LAMBCHOP was printed
across the top, and an address. It was
signed 'Stanley, USA.'

Sarah

It was two nights before Christmas, and all through the house not a Lambchop was stirring, but something was.

Stanley Lambchop sat up in his bed. 'Listen! Someone said "Rat."'

'It was more like "grat,"' said his younger brother Arthur, from his bed. 'In the living room, I think.'

The brothers tiptoed down the stairs.

For a moment all was silence in the darkened living room. Then came a *thump*.

'Ouch!' said a small voice. 'Drat again!'

'Are you a burglar?' Arthur called. 'Did you hurt yourself?'

'I am *not* a burglar!' said the voice. 'Where's the – ah!' The lights came on.

The brothers stared.

Before the fireplace, by the Christmas tree, stood a slender, dark-haired little girl wearing a red jacket and skirt, both trimmed with white fur.

'I banged it *twice*,' she said, rubbing her knee. 'Coming down the chimney, and just now.'

'We *do* have a front door, you know,' said Stanley.

'Well, so does my house. But, you know, this time of year . . .?' The girl sounded a bit nervous. 'Actually, I've never done this before. Let's see . . . Ha, ha, ha! Season's Greetings! Ha, ha, ha!'

'"Ha, ha!" to you,' said Arthur. 'What's so funny?'

'Funny?' said the girl. 'Oh! "Ho, ho, ho!" I meant. I'm Sarah Christmas. Who are you?'

'Arthur Lambchop,' said Arthur. 'That's my brother Stanley.'

'It is? But he's not *flat*.'

'He was, but I blew him up,' Arthur explained. 'With a bicycle pump.'

'Oh, no! I wish you hadn't.' Sarah Christmas sank into a chair. 'Drat! It's all going wrong! Perhaps I shouldn't have come. But that's how I am. Headstrong, my mother says. She –'

'Excuse me,' Stanley said. 'But where are you from?'

'And why *did* you come?' said Arthur.

Sarah told them.

Mr and Mrs Lambchop were reading in bed.

A tap came at the door, and then Stanley's voice. 'Hey! Can I come in?'

Mr and Mrs Lambchop cared greatly for proper speech. 'Hay is for horses, Stanley,' she said. 'And not "can" dear. You *may* come in.'

Stanley came in.

'What is the explanation, my boy, of this late call?' said Mr Lambchop, remembering past surprises. 'You have not, I see, become flat again. Has a genie come to visit? Or

11

perhaps the President of the United States has called?'

Mrs Lambchop smiled. 'You are very amusing, George.'

'Arthur and I were in bed,' said Stanley. 'But we heard a noise and went to see. It was a girl called Sarah Christmas, from Snow City. She talks a lot. She says her father says he won't come this year, but Sarah thinks he might change his mind if I ask him to. Because I wrote him a letter once that he liked. She wants me to go with her to Snow City. In her father's sleigh. It's at the North Pole, I think.' Stanley caught his breath. 'I said I'd have to ask you first.'

'Quite right,' said Mrs Lambchop.

Mr Lambchop went to the bathroom and drank a glass of water to calm himself.

'Now then, Stanley,' he said, returning. 'You have greatly startled us. Surely –'

'Put on your robe, George,' said Mrs Lambchop. 'Let us hear for ourselves what this visitor has to say.'

'This is *delicious*!' Sarah Christmas sipped the hot chocolate Mrs Lambchop had served them all. 'My mother makes it too, with cinnamon in it. And little cookies with –' Her glance had fallen on the mantelpiece. 'What's *that*, pinned up there?'

'Christmas stockings,' Stanley said. 'The blue one's mine.'

'But the other, the great square thing?'

'It's a pillow case.' Arthur blushed. 'My stocking wouldn't do. I have very small feet.'

'Pooh!' Sarah laughed. 'You wanted extra gifts, so –'

'Sarah, dear,' Mrs Lambchop said. 'Your father? Has he truly made up his mind, you think?'

'Oh, yes!' Sarah sighed. 'But I thought – Stanley being flat, that *really* interested him. I mean, I couldn't be *sure*, but if nobody ever did anything without –'

'You seem a very nice girl, Sarah.' Mr Lambchop gave a little laugh. 'But you *have* been joking with us, surely? I –'

The phone rang, and he answered it.

'Hello, George,' the caller said. 'This is your neighbour, Frank Smith. I know it's late, but I must congratulate you on your Christmas lawn display! Best –'

'Lawn?' said Mr Lambchop. 'Display?'

'The sleigh! And those life-like *reindeer*! What makes them move about like that? Batteries, I suppose?'

'Just a moment, Frank.' Mr Lambchop went to the window and looked out, Mrs Lambchop beside him.

'My goodness!' she said. 'One, two, three, four . . . eight! And such a pretty sleigh!'

Mr Lambchop returned to the phone. 'They *are* life-like, aren't they? Goodbye. Thank you for calling, Frank.'

'See? I'm not a joking kind of person, actually,' said Sarah Christmas. 'Now!

My idea *might* work, even without the flatness. Do let Stanley go!'

'To the North Pole?' said Mrs Lambchop. 'At night? By himself? Good gracious, Sarah!'

'It's not fair, asking Stanley, but not me,' said Arthur, feeling hurt. 'It's always like this! I never –'

'Oh, pooh!' Sarah Christmas smiled. 'Actually . . . You could *all* go. It's a very big sleigh.'

Mr and Mrs Lambchop looked at each other, then at Stanley and Arthur, then at each other again.

'Stanley just might make a difference, George,' Mrs Lambchop said. 'And if we can *all* go . . . ?'

'Quite right,' said Mr Lambchop. 'Sarah, we will accompany you to Snow City!'

'Hooray!' shouted Stanley and Arthur, and Sarah too.

Mrs Lambchop thought they should wait until Frank Smith had gone to bed. 'Imagine the gossip,' she said, 'were he to see our reindeer fly away.'

Mr Lambchop called his office to leave a message on the night-time answering machine. He would not be in tomorrow, he said, as he had been called unexpectedly out of town.

'There!' cried Stanley, by the window. 'The Smiths' light is out.'

The Lambchops changed quickly from pyjamas to warmer clothing, and followed Sarah to the sleigh.

The Sleigh

'Welcome aboard!' said Sarah, from the driver's seat.

The Lambchops, sitting on little benches that made the big sleigh resemble a roofless bus, could scarcely contain their excitement.

The night sky shone bright with stars, and from the windows of nearby houses red and green Christmas lights twinkled over snowy lawns and streets. Before them, the eight reindeer, fur shiny in the moonlight, tossed their antlered heads.

'Ready when you are, Sarah,' Mr Lambchop said.

'Good!' Sarah cleared her throat. 'Fasten your seat belts, please! We are about to depart for Snow City. My name is Sarah – I guess you know that – and I'll be glad to answer any questions you may have. Please do not move about without permission of the Sleigh Master – that's me, at least right now – and obey whatever instructions may –'

'Puleeese!' said Arthur.

'Oh, all right!' The Lambchops fastened their seat belts, and Sarah took up the reins. 'Ready, One? Ready, Two, Three –'

'Just *numbers*?' cried Mrs Lambchop.

'Why, we know such lovely reindeer names! Dasher, Dancer, Prancer, Vixen –'

'Comet, Cupid, Donder, Blitzen!' shouted Arthur. 'They're from a poem we know!'

'Those *are* good names!' said Sarah. 'Ready, One through Eight?'

The reindeer pawed the ground, jingling their harness bells.

'Now!' said Sarah.

The jingling stopped suddenly, and a great silence fell.

Now a silver mist rose, swirling, about the sleigh. The startled Lambchops could see nothing beyond the mist, not their house nor the houses of their neighbours, not the twinkling Christmas lights, not the bright stars above. There was only the silver mist, everywhere, cool against their cheeks.

'What is this, Sarah?' Mrs Lambchop called. 'Are we not to proceed to Snow City?'

Sarah's voice came cheerfully through the mist. 'We have proceeded. We're there!'

Snow City

Beyond the mist, excited voices rose. 'Sarah's back! . . . With strangers! Big ones! . . . Where's she been?'

'Poppa's elves,' said Sarah's voice. As she spoke, the mist swirled, then vanished as suddenly as it had come. Above them, the stars shone bright again.

The sleigh rested now in a snow-covered square, in front of a pretty red-roofed house. All about the square were tiny cottages, their windows aglow with light.

Elves surrounded the sleigh. 'Who *are* these people? . . . Is it true, what we've heard? . . . Ask Sarah! She'll know!'

The Lambchops smiled and waved. The elves seemed much like ordinary men and women, except that they had pointy ears, very wrinkled faces, and were only about half as tall as Arthur. All wore leather breeches or skirts with wide pockets from which tools and needles stuck out.

'Miss Sarah!' came a voice. 'Is it true? He won't go this year?'

Sarah hesitated. 'Well, sort of . . . But perhaps the Lambchops here . . . Be patient. Go home, please!'

The elves straggled off toward their cottages, grumbling. 'Not going? . . . Hah!

After all our work? . . . The *Who*chops? . . . I'd go work somewhere else, but *where*?'

A plump lady in an apron bustled out of the red-roofed house. 'Sarah! Are you all right? Going off like that! Though we did find your note. Gracious! Are those *all* Lambchops, dear?'

'I'm fine, Momma!' said Sarah. 'They wouldn't let Stanley come by himself. That's Stanley, there. The other one's Arthur. Stanley *was* flat, but he got round again.'

'Clever!' said Mrs Christmas. 'Well! Do all come in! Are you fond of hot chocolate?'

'. . . an excellent plan, I do see that. But – Oh, he's in *such* a state! And with Stanley no longer flat . . .' Mrs Christmas sighed. 'More chocolate, Lambchops?

I add a dash of cinnamon. Tasty, yes?'

'Delicious,' said Mrs Lambchop.

Everyone sat silent, sipping.

Mr Lambchop felt the time had come. 'May we see him now, Mrs Christmas? We should be getting home. So much to do, this time of year.'

'You forget where you are, George,' said Mrs Lambchop. 'Mrs Christmas, surely, is aware of the demands of the season.'

'I'm sorry about not being flat,' Stanley said. 'I did get tired of it, though.'

'No need to apologise,' said Mrs Christmas. 'Flat, round, whatever, people must be what shape they wish.'

'So true,' said Mrs Lambchop. 'But will your husband agree?'

'We shall see. Come.' Mrs Christmas rose, and the Lambchops followed her down the hall.

Mrs Christmas knocked on a door. 'Visitors, dear! From America.'

'Send 'em back!' said a deep voice.

'Sir?' Mr Lambchop tried to sound cheerful. 'A few minutes, perhaps? "'Tis the season to be jolly", eh? We –'

'Bah!' said the voice. 'Go home!'

'What a terrible temper!' Stanley said. 'He doesn't want to meet us at all!'

'I already *have* met him once,' Arthur whispered. 'In a department store.'

'That wasn't the real one, dear,' Mrs Lambchop said.

'Too bad,' said Arthur. 'He was much nicer than this one.'

Sarah stepped forward. 'Poppa? Can you hear me, Poppa?'

'I hear you, all right!' said the deep

voice. 'Took the Great Sleigh without permission, didn't you? Rascal!'

'The letter on your wall, Poppa?' Sarah said. 'The Lambchop letter? Well, they're *here*, the whole family! It wasn't easy, Poppa! I went down their chimney and scraped my knee, and then I banged it, the *same* knee, when I –'

'SARAH!' said the voice.

Sarah hushed, and so did everyone else.

'The flat boy, eh?' said the voice. 'Hmmmm . . .'

Mrs Lambchop took a comb from her bag and tidied Arthur's hair. Mr Lambchop straightened Stanley's collar.

'Come in!' said the voice behind the door.

Sarah's Father

The room was very dark, but it was possible to make out a desk at the far side, and someone seated behind it.

The Lambchops held their breaths. This was perhaps the most famous person in the world!

'Guess what, Poppa?' said Sarah, sounding quite nervous. 'The Lambchops know *names* for our reindeer!'

No answer came.

'Names, Poppa, not just *numbers*! There's Dashes and Frances and –'

'Dasher,' said Stanley. 'Then Dancer, then –'

'*Then* Frances!' cried Sarah. 'Or is it *Prances*? Then –'

'Waste of time, this!' said the figure behind the desk. But then a switch

clicked, and lights came on.

The Lambchops stared.

Except for a large TV in one corner
and a speaker-box on the desk, the room
was much like Mr Lambchop's study
at home. There were bookshelves and
comfortable chairs. Framed letters, one
of them Stanley's, hung behind the desk,
along with photographs of Mrs Christmas,

Sarah, and elves and reindeer, singly and in groups.

Sarah's father was large and stout, but otherwise not what they had expected.

He wore a blue zip jacket with 'N. Pole Athletic Club' lettered across it, and sat with his feet, in fuzzy brown slippers, up on the desk. His long white hair and beard were in need of trimming, and the beard had crumbs in it. On the desk, along with his feet, were a plate of cookies, a bowl of potato chips, and a bottle of strawberry soda with a straw in it.

'George Lambchop, sir,' said Mr Lambchop. 'Good evening. May I present my wife Harriet, and our sons Stanley and Arthur?'

'How do you do.' Sarah's father sipped his soda. 'Whichever is Stanley, step forward, please, and turn about.'

Stanley stepped forward and turned about.

'You're *round*, boy!'

'I blew him up,' said Arthur. 'With a bicycle pump.'

Sarah's father raised his eyebrows. 'Very funny. Very funny indeed.' He ate some potato chips. 'Well? What brings you all here?'

Mr Lambchop cleared his throat. 'I understand, Mr — No, that can't be right. What *is* the proper form of address?'

'Depends where you're from. "Santa" is the American way. But I'm known also as Father Christmas, *Père Noel*, *Babbo Natale*, *Julenisse* . . . Little country, way off somewhere, they call me "The Great Hugga Wagoo."'

'Hugga Wagoo?' Arthur laughed loudly, and Mrs Lambchop shook her head at him.

Mr Lambchop continued, 'We understand, sir – *Santa*, if I may? – that you propose not to make your rounds this year? We are here to ask that you reconsider.'

'Reconsider?' said Sarah's father. 'The way things are these days? Hah! See for yourselves!'

The big TV in the corner clicked on, and he switched from channel to channel.

The first channel showed battleships firing flaming missiles; the second, aeroplanes dropping bombs; the third, cars crashing other cars. Then came buildings burning, people begging for food, people hitting each other, people firing pistols at policemen. The last channel showed a game show, men and women in chicken

costumes grabbing for prizes in a pool of mud.

Sarah's father switched off the TV. 'Peace on Earth? Goodwill toward men? Been wasting my time, it seems!'

'You have been watching *far* too much television,' said Mrs Lambchop. 'No wonder you take a dim view of things.'

'Facts are facts, madam! Everywhere, violence and greed! Hah! Right here in my own office, a whole family come begging for Christmas treats!'

The Lambchops were deeply shocked.

'I'm greedy sometimes,' said Stanley. 'But not always.'

'I'm quite nice, actually,' Arthur said. 'And Stanley's even nicer than me.'

'*I*, dear,' said Mrs Lambchop. 'Nicer than I.'

Mr Lambchop, finding it hard to believe that he was at the North Pole having a conversation like this, chose his words with care.

'You misjudge us, sir,' he said. 'There is indeed much violence in the world, and selfishness. But not everyone – we Lambchops, for example –'

'Hah! Different, are you?' Sarah's father spoke into the little box on his desk. 'Yo! Elf Ewald?'

'Central Files,' said a voice from the box. 'Ewald here.'

'Ewald,' said Sarah's father. 'Check this year's letters, under "USA". Bring me the "Lambchop" file.'

The Letters

Elf Ewald had come and gone, leaving behind a large brown folder.

'Not greedy, Lambchops? We shall see!' Sarah's father drew a letter from the folder and read it aloud.

'"Dear Santa, My parents say I can't have a real car until I'm grown up. I want one now. A big red one. Make that two cars, both red." Hah! Hear that? Shameful!'

Mrs Lambchop shook her head. 'I should be interested,' she said, 'to learn who wrote that letter?'

'It is signed – Hmmmm . . . Frederic. Frederic Lampop.'

Stanley laughed. 'Our name's not "Lampop"! And we don't even know any Frederics!'

'Mistakes *do* happen, you know! I get *millions* of letters!' Sarah's father drew from the folder again. 'Ah! This one's from *you*!'

' "Dear Santa," ' he read. ' "I hope you are fine. I need lots of gifts this year. Shoes and socks and shirts and pants and underwear. And big tents. At least a hundred of each would be nice –" A hundred! *There's* greediness!'

'It does seem a bit much, Stanley,'

said Mr Lambchop. 'And why tents, for goodness sake?'

'You'll see,' said Stanley.

Sarah's father read on. '". . . of each would be nice. But not delivered to my house. It was on TV about a terrible earthquake in South America where all the houses fell down, and people lost all their clothes and don't have anywhere to live. Please take everything to where the earthquake was. Thank you. Your friend, Stanley Lambchop. PS. I would send my old clothes, but they are mostly from when I was flat and wouldn't fit anybody else."'

'Good for you, Stanley!' said Mrs Lambchop. 'A fine idea, the tents.'

'Hmmmph! One letter, that's all.' Sarah's father chose another letter. 'This one's got jam on it.'

'Excuse me,' said Arthur. 'I was eating a sandwich.'

'"Dear Santa,"' Sarah's father read, '"I have hung up a pillow case instead of a stocking –" Hah! The old pillow case trick!'

'Wait!' cried Arthur. 'Read the rest!'

'". . . instead of a stocking. Please fill this up with chocolate bars, my favourite kind with nuts. My brother Stanley is writing to you about an earthquake, and how people there need clothes and tents and things. Well, I think they need food too, and little stoves to cook on. So please give them the chocolate bars, and food and stoves. The bars should be the big kind. It doesn't matter about the nuts. Sincerely, Arthur Lambchop."'

Mrs Lambchop gave Arthur a little hug.

'All right, *two* letters,' said Sarah's father.
'But from brothers. Count as one, really.'

He took a last letter from the folder.
'Nice penmanship, this one . . . Mr and
Mrs George Lambchop! Now there's a
surprise!'

'Well, why *not*?' said Mrs Lambchop.

Mr Lambchop said, 'No harm, eh, just dropping a line?'

Their letter was read.

'"Dear Sir: Perhaps you expect letters from children only, since as people grow older they often begin to doubt that you truly exist. But when our two sons were very small, and asked if you were real, we said "yes". And if they were to ask again now, we would not say "no". We would say that you are not real, of course, for those who do not believe in you, but very real indeed for those who *do*. Our Christmas wish is that you will never have cause to doubt that Stanley and Arthur Lambchop, and their parents, take the latter position. Sincerely, Mr and Mrs George Lambchop, USA."'

Sarah's father thought for a moment.

'Hmmm . . . *Latter* position? Ah? *Do* believe. I see.'

'See, Poppa?' said Sarah. 'No greediness! Not one −'

'Fine letters, Sarah. I agree.' There was sadness in the deep voice now. 'But all, Sarah, from the same family that thought to deceive me with that "flatness" story. Flat indeed!'

Mrs Lambchop gasped. 'Deceive? Oh, no!'

'Round is round, madam.' Sarah's father shook his head. 'The lad's shape speaks for itself.'

The hearts of all the Lambchops sank within them. Their mission had failed, they thought. For millions and millions of children all over the world, a joyful holiday

was lost, perhaps never to come again.

Arthur felt especially bad. It was his fault, he told himself, for thinking of that bicycle pump.

Stanley felt worst of all. If only he hadn't grown tired of being flat, hadn't let Arthur blow him round again! If only there were proof –

And then he remembered something.

'Wait!' he shouted, and stood on tiptoe to whisper in Mrs Lambchop's ear.

'What . . .?' she said. 'I can't – The *what*? Oh! Yes! I had forgotten! Good for you, Stanley!'

Rummaging in her bag, she found her wallet, from which she drew a photograph. She gave it to Sarah's father.

'Do keep that,' she said. 'We have more at home.'

The snapshot had been taken by Mr Lambchop the day after the big bulletin board fell on Stanley. It showed him, quite flat, sliding under a  closed door. Only his top half was visible, smiling up at the camera. The bottom half was still behind the door.

For a long moment, as Sarah's father studied the picture, no one spoke.

'My apologies, Lambchops,' he said at last. 'Flat he is. *Was*, anyhow. I've half a mind to –' He sighed. 'But those red cars, asking for *two*, that –'

'That was Lam*POP*!' cried Arthur. 'Not –'

'Just teasing, lad!'

Sarah's father had jumped up, a great smile on his face.

'Yo, elves!' he shouted into his speaker phone. 'Prepare to load gifts! Look lively! Tomorrow is Christmas Eve, you know!'

The next moments were joyful indeed.

'Thank you, thank you! . . . Hooray! . . . Hooray! . . . Hooray!' shouted Mr and Mrs Lambchop, and Stanley and Arthur and Sarah.

Sarah's mother kissed everyone. Mrs Lambchop kissed Sarah's father, and almost fainted when she realised what she had done.

Then Sarah's father asked Stanley to autograph the sliding-under-the-door picture, and when Stanley had written 'All best wishes, S. Lambchop' across the picture, he pinned it to the wall.

'Blew him round, eh?' he said to Arthur. 'Like to have seen that!'

He turned to Sarah. 'Come, my dear! While I freshen up, teach me those reindeer names. Then I will see our visitors safely home!'

Going Home

A crowd of elves had gathered with Mrs
Christmas and Sarah to say goodbye. 'Bless
you, Lambchops!' they called. 'Thank
goodness you came! . . . Think if you
hadn't! . . . Whew! . . . Farewell, farewell!'

In the Great Sleigh, Sarah's father took
up the reins. 'Ready, Lambchops?'

He made a fine appearance now, his hair
and beard combed, and wearing a smart

green cloak and cap. The famous red suit, he had explained, was reserved for delivering gifts.

'Goodbye, everyone!' called Mrs Lambchop. 'We will remember you always!'

'You bet!' cried Stanley. 'I'll *never* forget!'

'But you will, dear,' said Mrs Christmas. 'You will *all* forget.'

'Hardly.' Mr Lambchop smiled. 'An evening like this does not slip one's mind.'

'Poppa will see to it, actually,' said

Sarah. 'Snow City, all of us here . . .
We're supposed to be, you know, sort of
a mystery. Isn't that *silly*? I mean, if –'

'Sarah!' her father said. 'We must go.'

The Lambchops looked up at the night
sky, still bright with stars, then turned for
a last sight of the little red-roofed house
behind them, and of the elves' cottages
about the snowy square.

'We are ready,' said Mr Lambchop.

'Goodbye, goodbye!' called Mrs Lambchop and Stanley and Arthur.

'Goodbye, goodbye!' called the elves, waving.

The eight reindeer tossed their heads, jingling their harness bells. One bell flew off, and Stanley caught the little silver cup in his hand. Suddenly, as before, the jingling stopped, all was silence, and the pale mist rose again about the sleigh.

Sarah's father's voice rang clear. 'Come, Dasher, Dancer, Prancer, Vixen! Come, Comet, Cupid, Donder and . . . oh, whatsisname?'

'Blitzen!' Stanley called.

'Thank you. Come, Blitzen!'

The mist swirled, closing upon the sleigh.

Christmas

The Lambchops all remarked the next morning on how soundly they had slept, and how late. Mr Lambchop ate breakfast in a rush.

'Will you be all day at the office, George?' Mrs Lambchop asked. 'It *is* Christmas Eve, you know.'

'There is much to do,' said Mr Lambchop. 'I will be kept late, I'm afraid.'

But there was little to occupy him at his office, since a practical joker had left word he would not be in. He was home by noon to join friends and family for carol singing about the neighbourhood.

Mrs Lambchop had the carolers in for hot chocolate, which was greatly admired. She had added cinnamon, she explained; the idea had just popped into her head. The carolers were all very jolly, and Frank Smith, who lived next door, made everyone laugh, the Lambchops hardest of all, by claiming he had seen reindeer on their lawn the night before.

On Christmas morning, they opened their gifts to each other, and gifts from relatives and friends. Then came a surprise for Stanley and Arthur. Mr Lambchop had just turned on the TV news.

'. . . and now a flash from South America, from where the earthquake was,' the announcer was saying. 'Homeless villagers here are giving thanks this morning for a tremendous supply of socks, shirts, underwear, and food. They have also received a *thousand* tents, and a *thousand* little stoves to cook on!' The screen showed a homeless villager, looking grateful. 'The tents, and the little stoves,'

the villager said. 'Just what we need! Bless whoever sends these tents and stoves! Also the many tasty chocolate bars with nuts!'

'He's blessing *me*!' cried Stanley. 'I asked for tents in my letter. But I wasn't sure it would work.'

'Well, *I* wrote about stoves,' Arthur said. '*And* chocolate bars. But they didn't have to have nuts.'

Happy coincidences! thought Mr and Mrs Lambchop, smiling at each other.

Christmas dinner, shared with various aunts, uncles, and cousins, was an enormous meal of turkey, yams, and three kinds of pie. Then everyone went ice-skating in the park. By bedtime, Stanley and Arthur were more than ready for sleep.

'A fine holiday,' said Mr Lambchop, tucking Arthur in.

'Yes indeed.' Mrs Lambchop tucked in Stanley. 'Pleasant dreams, boys, and – What's this?' She had found something on the table by his bed. 'Why, it's a little bell! A silver bell!'

'It was in my pocket,' Stanley said. 'I don't know what it's from.'

'Pretty. Goodnight, you two,' said Mrs Lambchop, and switched off the light.

The brothers lay silent for a moment in the dark.

'Stanley . . .?' Arthur said. 'It *was* a nice holiday, don't you think.'

'*Extra* nice,' said Stanley. 'But why? It's as if I have something wonderful to remember, but can't think what.'

'Me too. Merry Christmas, Stanley.'

'Merry Christmas, Arthur,' said Stanley,
and soon they were both asleep.

FLAT STANLEY

Stanley, Flat Again

A Morning Surprise

Mrs Lambchop was making breakfast. Mr Lambchop, at the kitchen table, helped by reading bits from the morning paper.

'Here's an odd one, Harriet,' he said. 'There's a chicken in Sweden that rides a bike.'

'So do I, George,' said Mrs Lambchop, not really listening.

'Listen to this. "Merker Building now

empty. To be collapsed next week."
Imagine! Eight floors!'

'Poor thing!' Mrs Lambchop set out plates. 'My, isn't this a lovely sunny morning!' She raised her voice. 'Boys! Breakfast is ready!'

Her glance fell upon a row of photographs on the wall above the sink. There was a smiling Stanley, only half an inch thick, his big bulletin board having fallen from the bedroom wall to rest upon him overnight. Next came reminders of the many family adventures that had come after Stanley's younger brother, Arthur, had cleverly blown him round again with a bicycle pump. There were the brothers with Prince Haraz, the young genie who

had granted wishes for them all after being accidentally summoned by Stanley from a lamp. There was the entire family with Santa Claus and his daughter, Sarah, taken during a Christmas visit to the North Pole. There was the family again in Washington, DC, in the office of the President of the United States, who had asked them to undertake a secret mission into outer space. The last picture showed Arthur standing beside a balloon on which Mrs Lambchop had painted a picture of Stanley's face. The balloon, its string in fact held by Stanley, had been a valuable guide to his presence, since he was invisible at the time. 'Boys!' she called again. 'Breakfast!'

In their bedroom, Stanley and Arthur had finished dressing.

While Stanley filled his backpack, Arthur bounced a tennis ball. 'Let's go,' he said. 'Here! Catch!'

Stanley had just reached for a book on the shelf by his bed. The ball struck his back as he turned, and he banged his shoulder on a corner of the shelf.

'Ouch!'

'Sorry,' Arthur said. 'But let's go, okay? You know how long – STANLEY!'

'Why are you shouting?' Stanley adjusted his pack. 'C'mon! I'm so hungry –' He paused. 'Oh, boy! Arthur, do you see?'

'I do, actually.' Arthur swallowed hard. 'You're, you know . . . flat.'

The brothers stared at each other.

'The pump?' Stanley said. 'It might work again.'

Arthur fetched the bicycle pump from their toy chest and Stanley lay on the bed with the hose end in his mouth.

Arthur gave a long, steady, pump.

Stanley made a face. 'That hurts!'

Arthur pumped again, and Stanley snatched the hose from his mouth. 'Owww! That really hurts! It wasn't like that before. We'd better stop.'

'Now what?' Arthur said. 'We can't just hide in here forever, you know.'

Mrs Lambchop's call came again. 'Boys! Please come!'

'Do me a favour,' Stanley said. 'You tell

them. Sort of get them ready, okay?'

'Okay,' said Arthur, and went to tell.

Arthur stood in the kitchen doorway. 'Hey, guess what?' he said.

'Hay is for horses, dear,' said Mrs Lambchop. 'Good morning! Breakfast is ready.'

'School, Arthur,' Mr Lambchop said from behind his newspaper. 'Where's Stanley?'

'Guess what?' Arthur said again.

Mrs Lambchop sighed. 'Oh, all right! I can't guess. Tell.'

'Stanley's flat again,' said Arthur.

Mr Lambchop put down his paper.

Mrs Lambchop closed her eyes. 'Flat

again? Is that what you said?'

'Yes,' said Arthur.

'It's true.' Stanley stood now beside Arthur in the doorway. 'Just look.'

'Good grief!' said Mr Lambchop. 'I can't

believe that bulletin board –'

'It didn't fall on me this time,' Stanley said. 'I just got flat. Arthur tried to pump

me up, like before, but it hurt too much.'

'Oh, Stanley!' Mrs Lambchop ran to kiss him. 'How do you feel now?'

'Fine, actually,' Stanley said. 'Just surprised. Can I go to school?'

Mrs Lambchop thought for a moment. 'Very well. Eat your breakfast. After school we'll hear what Dr Dan has to say.'

Dr Dan

'Ah, Mr and Mrs Lambchop! And the boys!' said Dr Dan as they entered his office. 'How nice to –'

His eyes widened. 'Good heavens, Stanley! Mr Lambchop, you really must do something about that bulletin board!'

'It is still firmly in place, Dr Dan,' Mrs Lambchop said. 'We are at a loss to account for this attack of flatness.'

'Hmm.' Dr Dan thought for a moment. 'Is there, perhaps, a family history of flatness?'

'No,' Mr Lambchop said. 'We'd remember that.'

'We got dressed for school,' Stanley explained. 'We didn't even have breakfast. And all of a sudden, I got flat.'

Dr Dan frowned. 'Nothing happened? Nothing at all?'

'Well, Arthur hit me with a tennis ball,' Stanley said. 'And then I banged my shoulder on –'

'Aha!' Jumping up, Dr Dan took a large book from the case behind his desk and began turning pages. 'This is Dr Franz

Gemeister's excellent *Difficult and Peculiar Cases*. Just let me find . . . Here it is! "Flatness," page two seventeen!'

He read aloud. '"Sudden flatness . . . extremely rare . . . minimal documentation . . . hearsay reports . . ." Ah, here it is! "Account dating back to mid-fifth century AD. During battle, Mongo the Fierce, an aide to Attila the Hun, was struck twice, simultaneously, from behind, and at once became no thicker than his shield. He became known as Mongo the Plate, and lived to old age without regaining his original girth.'"

Dr Dan closed the book. 'As I suspected! The OBP.'

'Beg pardon?' said Mrs Lambchop.

'The OBP. Osteal Balance Point,' Dr Dan explained. 'A little known anatomical feature. The human body, of course, is a complex miracle, its skeleton a delicate framework of supports and balances. The Osteal Balance Point may occur almost anywhere in the upper torso. It is vulnerable only to the application of simultaneous pressures at two points which vary depending on the age and particular "design," let us say, of the individual involved. In my opinion, the pressures created by the tennis ball and the shelf corner affected Stanley's OBP, thereby turning him flat.'

For a moment, everyone was silent.

'The first time Stanley went flat, you were greatly puzzled by his condition,' Mr Lambchop said at last. 'Now you seem remarkably well informed.'

'I read up on it,' said Dr Dan.

Mrs Lambchop sighed. 'Perhaps we should seek a second opinion. Who is the world's leading authority on the OBP?'

'That would be me,' said Dr Dan.

'I see . . . Well, we've taken enough of your time.' Mr Lambchop rose, motioning his family to follow. 'Thank you, Dr Dan.'

At the door, Mrs Lambchop turned. 'Perhaps if we found the, you know, the OBP, we could make Stanley –'

'No, no!' said Dr Dan. 'It would be

dangerous to put the lad through such a skeletal strain again! And finding the OBP? Not very likely, I'm afraid.'

Arthur had an idea. 'I know! If we all got sticks and hit Stanley all over at the same time, and kept doing it, then –'

'That will do, Arthur,' Mr Lambchop said, and led his family out.

Stanley Sails

Early the next Sunday morning, Mr Lambchop had a call from an old college friend. Ralph Jones.

'Just wanted to remind you, George, that Stanley and I have a date to go sailing today,' he said.

'He's looking forward to it, Ralph.' Mr Lambchop hesitated. 'I should mention, perhaps, that Stanley has gone flat again.'

Mr Jones sighed. 'I thought he'd got over that. Well, I'll pick him up at ten.'

Later that morning, driving with Stanley to his sailing club on the seashore, Mr Jones inquired about a foreign visitor he had once met with the Lambchops. 'A prince, yes? He around these days?'

Stanley knew he meant the young genie, Prince Haraz, but it would be difficult to explain not only the genie part, but also that Haraz had returned to the genie kingdom from which he had come.

'No,' Stanley said. 'He went home, actually.'

'Too bad.' Mr Jones was famous for his amazing memory. 'Haraz, as I recall.

Prince Fawzi Mustafa Aslan Mirza Malek Namerd Haraz?'

'Right,' said Stanley.

In the harbour of the sailing club, Mr Jones prepared his boat, *Lovebug*, and explained it to Stanley. 'This big sail here is the mainsail, and that's the rudder back there, for steering. In this zip bag is another sail, called a spinnaker. We'll use that one for extra speed when we're running before the wind. See that boat way out there, how its spinnaker is puffing out front?'

Stanley laughed. The spinnaker looked like an open umbrella lying on its side.

'See over there,' Mr Jones went on, 'between the committee boat, with the judges on it, and the red buoy? That's the starting line. The race ends back there too. First boat to cross that line wins!'

He cast off the mooring line, and the mainsail filled. *Lovebug* headed out to join the other boats.

Mr Jones pointed. 'There! That's Jasper Green's boat, *Windswept*. He's the one I want especially to beat!'

'Why? Are you mad at him?' Stanley asked.

'He was very rude to me once. But never mind. Let's just make sure we win!'

Behind the start line, they found themselves beside *Windswept*. Jasper Green gave a friendly wave, but Ralph Jones ignored him.

'You're always in a bad mood with me, Ralph,' Mr Green said. 'Why? I don't – Here we go!'

A pistol shot had signalled the start of the race. *Lovebug* and *Windswept* and the other racers glided across the start line behind the motor-powered committee boat, which led them along a course marked by buoys with bright green streamers.

Stanley sat back, enjoying himself. The sun was bright, the breeze fresh against his face, the sky clear and blue, the water a beautiful slate colour. There were boats on both sides of them, boats ahead, boats behind. How pretty they were, their white sails making cheerful crackling sounds as they billowed in the wind!

Along the shore, people waved from the porches of houses, their voices carrying faintly on the wind. 'Way to go! . . . Looking good, sailors! . . . Looking flat, one of them!' Stanley waved back, knowing that the teasing was kindly meant.

Lovebug passed other boats, but there were many more still ahead. And now they were almost abreast of *Windswept*. Stanley saw that Jasper Green had hoisted his spinnaker, and that other boats had too.

'I've got you beat, Ralph!' Jasper Green shouted.

'We'll just round this point, Stanley! Then – Now!' exclaimed Ralph Jones.

'Let's show Jasper what running before the wind really means!'

He attached his spinnaker to a halyard and ran it up the mast. *Who-o-oosh*! The spinnaker billowed out, and Stanley felt *Lovebug* surge forward, as if pushed by an invisible hand.

'Here we go!' shouted Ralph Jones.

They passed five more boats, three more, then *Windswept*! They were ahead of everyone now, and the finish line lay ahead!

'We're going to win!' Stanley shouted.

'Yes!' Ralph Jones shouted back. 'Just wait till Jasper –'

R-i-i-i-i-p!

The sound came from above. Looking up, they saw that the top of the spinnaker had torn.

R-i-i-i-i-i-i-p!

The rip streaked downward, and now the spinnaker, torn all the way down, flapped uselessly in the wind. *Lovebug* slowed.

'Drat!' Mr Jones did his best with the mainsail. 'Drat, drat, drat!'

Windswept came up behind them. 'Tough luck!' called Jasper Green. 'Ha, ha!'

'Drat!' Mr Jones sighed. 'Nothing we can do, Stanley. Unless – This may be crazy, but . . . Stanley, perhaps you could be our spinnaker?'

'What?' Stanley shouted. 'How?'

'Good question,' said Mr Jones. 'Let's see . . . First go take hold of the mast. Now maybe –'

'Excuse me,' Stanley said. 'But did you ever do this before?'

'Stanley, *nobody* ever did this before.' Mr Jones took a deep breath. 'Okay.' Now twist around to face forward, and grab the mast behind you above your head!'

Stanley did as he was told, planting his feet on the sides of the boat to hold him in place. The wind pressed him from behind, driving *Lovebug* toward the finish line.

'Yes! Chest forward! Butt back!' shouted Mr Jones. 'Best spinnaker I ever had!' In a moment they had passed *Windswept*, and Stanley could not help laughing at the surprise on Jasper Green's face.

And then they were across the finish line! *Lovebug* had won!

Back in the clubhouse, Jasper Green would not admit that he had lost. A flat person used as a sail? He had never seen *that* before, he said, and went to the race committee office to complain. But he returned shortly to report that *Lovebug* had indeed won. The committee had advised him, he said, that there was no rule against a crew member allowing the wind to blow against him.

'Great sailing, Ralph!' he said. 'I thought it was my race, I really did!'

'Thank you, Jasper,' Mr Jones said, but Stanley noticed that he did not smile.

Jasper Green noticed too. 'Ralph, you're still mad at me,' he said. 'But *why*?'

'You spilled coffee on my white pants,

Jasper,' said Ralph Jones. 'And you just laughed when I jumped up.'

'What?' Jasper Green seemed greatly surprised. 'I don't remember – Where? When?'

'We were having lunch,' said Mr Jones. 'At the old Vandercook Hotel.'

'The Vandercook? It closed down twenty years ago!' Mr Green slapped his forehead. 'I *do* remember! That lunch was twenty years ago, Ralph!'

'Twenty-one, actually.'

'All right, all right!' said Mr Green. 'I apologise, for heaven's sake!'

Ralph Jones smiled warmly. 'Perfectly all right, Jasper,' he said. 'Don't give it another thought.'

Back to School

Back at school, Stanley was pleased that his classmates, who still remembered his previous flatness, made no great fuss about it now. Mostly they expressed only cheerful interest. 'Feeling okay, Stan?' they said, and 'Lookin' sharp, man! Sharp, see? Get the joke?' Only mean Emma Weeks was unpleasant. 'Huh! Mr Show-off again!'

Emma said one day, but Stanley pretended not to hear.

He had been back at school for a week when a newspaper, learning of this unusally shaped student, sent a photographer to investigate. He found Stanley watching a practice on the football field.

'Flash Tobin,' he said. 'From the *Daily Sentinel*. You're the flat kid, right?'

Stanley thought he must be joking. 'How did you know?' he said, joking back.

'How did I –' The photographer laughed. 'Oh, I get it! Can I take your picture, kid? Right here by the goal posts?'

Stanley nodded, and Flash Tobin took his picture. 'I heard there was a flat kid here before,' he said. 'Helped catch sneak thieves at the Famous Museum of Art. But that kid, I heard he got round again.'

'It was me,' Stanley told him.

'You go back and forth, huh?' The photographer was impressed. 'Okay, get round now. I'd like a shot of that too.'

'I can't just do it when I want,' Stanley explained. 'The first time, my brother had to blow me up. With a bicycle pump.'

'Make a great picture!' Flash Tobin shook his head. 'Well, we'll just go with flat.'

Stanley's picture was in the *Daily Sentinel* the next morning, and Arthur could not help showing his jealousy. Stanley was always getting his picture in the paper, he said. Didn't they see how interesting it would be to have a picture of his brother?

There was a football team practice that afternoon, and the day was windy. It was worrisome, the coach said, the way Stanley got blown about. Perhaps, for the sake of the team, he should switch to an indoor sport.

Stanley loved football, and the more he thought about what the coach had said, the sadder he felt.

Miss Elliott, his form teacher, noticed that he was not his usual cheerful self. 'Mr Redfield, the new guidance counsellor, is said to be very helpful to troubled students,' she told him. 'Shall I ask him to find a time for you?'

'I guess,' Stanley said, and Miss Elliott spoke to him again after lunch. 'Such good luck, Stanley! Mr Redfield will see you right after school today!'

'Come in, Stanley. Sit right there!' Mr Redfield pointed to a comfortable chair.

Stanley sat, and Mr Redfield leaned

back behind his desk. 'Now then . . .
You do understand that anything you say
here is completely confidential? I won't
tell anybody.'

Stanley wondered what he could say
that would interest anybody else.

'Miss Elliott tells me you seem troubled.'
Mr Redfield lowered his voice. 'What's
wrong?'

'I'm not sure, actually,' Stanley said.

Mr Redfield picked up a pad and a pen.
'Speak freely. Whatever comes into your
head. Anything special happen lately?'

'Well, I got flat,' Stanley said.

Mr Redfield made a note on his pad. 'I do
see that, yes. How did that make you feel?'

Stanley thought for a moment. 'Flat.'

'I see.' Mr Redfield nodded. 'This flatness, it's come upon you before, I'm told. Is it possible that somehow, without even admitting it to yourself, you wanted it to happen again?'

'No way!' Stanley said firmly. 'The first time, it was kind of fun for a while. Flying like a kite, and being mailed to California, things like that. But then I got, you know, tired of it. And now I might get put off the football team.'

Mr Redfield nodded again. 'You take no pleasure now in your unusual shape?'

Stanley thought for a moment. 'Well, sometimes.' He told about being a sail, and helping Ralph Jones win a race.

Mr Redfield made another note. 'I see.

This dream of being a sail, have you dreamed it before?'

Stanley stared at him. 'It wasn't a . . . It really happened! I'm just tired of being different, I guess.'

Mr Redfield pressed his fingertips together. 'Different? How do you feel different, would you say?'

Stanley wondered how Mr Redfield could be a good guidance counsellor if he had both terrible eyesight and a terrible memory.

'Well, I'm the only one in my class who's flat,' he said. 'The whole school, actually.'

'Interesting.' Mr Redfield made another note and glanced at his watch. 'I'm afraid our time is up, Stanley. Would you like to see me again? Just let Miss Elliott know.'

'Okay,' Stanley said politely, but he didn't think he would.

Why Me?

Stanley had looked sad all evening, Arthur thought. At bedtime, as they lay waiting for Mr and Mrs Lambchop to come say good night, he wondered how to cheer his brother up.

It was raining hard, and he remembered suddenly the rainy evening that Stanley had snacked on raisins, and by morning had become invisible. A little-known consequence, Dr Dan had explained, of eating fruit during bad weather.

'Hear the rain, Stanley?' he said. 'Better not eat any fruit.'

'Ha, ha, ha.' Stanley sounded cross. 'Just leave me alone, okay?'

'Stanley's in a terrible mood,' Arthur told Mr and Mrs Lambchop when they came in. 'He won't even talk to me.'

'What's wrong, my boy?' Mr Lambchop asked.

'Nothing.' Stanley put his pillow over his head.

'If my picture was in the newspaper practically every day, I'd be happy,' Arthur said. 'I mean, why –'

Mrs Lambchop hushed him. 'Stanley, dear? What is troubling you?'

'Nothing. Nothing,' Stanley said from under the pillow, and sat up. 'But why me? Why am I always getting flat, or invisible or something? Why can't it just once be someone else?'

'I wouldn't mind, actually,' Arthur said. 'Just for a while. I —'

'Hush, Arthur!' Mrs Lambchop put out the overhead light, lit a corner lamp, and sat by Stanley on his bed. Mr Lambchop sat with Arthur. The gentle patter of the rain against the windows, the glow of the little lamp, made the bedroom cozy indeed.

'I do see what you mean, Stanley,' Mr Lambchop said at last. 'Why do these things happen to you? Your mother and I don't know the answer either. But things often happen without there seeming to be a reason, and then something else happens, and suddenly the first thing seems to have had a purpose after all.'

'Well put, George!' Mrs Lambchop squeezed Stanley's hand. 'What we do know, Stanley dear, is that we're very proud of you, and love you very much. And we understand about the flatness, and all the other unexpected happenings, how upsetting it must be.'

'It sure is!' said Stanley. 'How would you like never knowing when you might get flat? Or invisible? Maybe someday I'll wake up ten feet tall or one inch short, or

with green hair, or a tail or something!'

'I know . . .' Mrs Lambchop said softly, and Mr Lambchop came and patted Stanley's shoulder. Then they kissed both boys, switched off the lamp, and went out.

Arthur spoke into the darkened room. 'Stanley?'

'I'm trying to sleep,' said Stanley. 'What?'

'I was just thinking,' Arthur said. 'If you got invisible, and then you got flat, how would they know?'

'Huh? I don't –' Stanley laughed. 'Oh, I get it! About the flatness. Good one, Arthur.'

Arthur laughed too.

'Quiet, please,' said Stanley. 'I'm trying to sleep.'

'Okay,' Arthur said, but he chuckled several times before he fell asleep.

Emma

Mr Lambchop came home early the next afternoon, full of excitement.

'Guess what?' he said. 'The old Merker Department Store? Eight floors, all emptied out, waiting to be torn down? Well, last night most of it fell down by itself!'

He switched on the TV. 'News time! Let's get the latest!'

'. . . more on the Merker Building collapse!' a newscaster was saying. 'It's just a mountain of rubble now, folks! Three workmen have been treated for minor bruises, but no other injuries are reported. The public is requested to avoid the area until –'

A young woman ran on, handed him a slip of paper, and ran off again.

'Hold on! This just in!' The newscaster read from the slip. 'Wow! A little girl is trapped under all that wreckage! Emma Weeks, daughter of local businessman Oswald Weeks!'

'Emma Weeks!' Stanley exclaimed. 'She's in my class! No wonder she wasn't at school today!'

'Emma's not hurt, it appears,' the newscaster continued. 'Firemen called to the scene can hear her calling up through chinks in the wreckage, demanding food and water! But Fire Chief Johnson has forbidden any rescue efforts! Any disturbance, any shifting of the wreckage, he says, might bring the rest of the building crashing down! Now, here's Tom Miller!'

The TV screen showed a reporter with a microphone standing by the wrecked building.

'Emma Weeks!' shouted the reporter, holding his microphone up to a crack. 'Do you hear me? Are you all right?'

Emma's voice was faint but clear. 'Oh, sure! I'm just great! I hope a building falls on me every day, you know? C'mon, get me out of here!'

Mrs Lambchop sighed. 'Such an unfortunate tone! She is under great strain, of course.'

'Emma's always like that,' Stanley said.

Half an hour later, while Mrs Lambchop was preparing supper, a siren sounded outside, then died away. Opening the front door, Mr Lambchop saw a Fire Department car at the curb. On the doorstep stood Fire Chief Johnson and a very worried-looking man and woman.

'Mr Lambchop?' said Chief Johnson. 'I'll get right to the point, sir. I reckon you heard about little Emma Weeks, trapped

in the Merker wreck? Well, Mr and Mrs Weeks here, and me, we'd like a word with you folks.'

'Of course!' Mr Lambchop led the visitors into the house and introduced them to Mrs Lambchop and Stanley and Arthur.

'Oh, Mrs Weeks!' Mrs Lambchop cried. 'Your poor daughter! You must be dreadfully worried!'

'We are indeed!' said Mr Weeks. 'But Chief Johnson thinks your Stanley might be able to save Emma!'

'Who, me?' and 'Who, Stanley?' said Stanley and Arthur.

Chief Johnson explained. 'Problem is that if a policeman, or one of my firemen, tries to dig his way in to Emma, the whole rest of the building could crash down on 'em! Too bad we don't have a flat fireman, I was thinking. Flat fella could squeeze through all those narrow openings we know are there, 'cause we hear Emma when she calls. Then I recollected the newspaper story, with a picture of Stanley here. Hit me right away! That boy could maybe wiggle in to Emma!'

For a moment, everyone was silent. Then Mrs Lambchop shook her head.

'It sounds terribly dangerous,' she said. 'I'm sorry, but I must say no.'

'It is a tad risky, ma'am,' said Chief Johnson. 'But we've got to remember the boy is already flat.'

Mrs Weeks sobbed. 'Oh, poor Emma!

How are we to save her?'

Mrs Lambchop bit her lip.

Stanley remembered something. 'I was just thinking.' He turned to Mr Lambchop. 'The other night? When I got mad about all the crazy things that keep happening to me? Remember what you said? You said that sometime things happen that nobody can see a reason for, and then afterwards some other thing happens, and all of a sudden it seems like the first thing had a reason after all. Well, I was just thinking that me getting flat again was one crazy thing, and that maybe Emma getting stuck where I'm the only one who can try to save her, that might be the second thing.'

Mr Lambchop nodded, and took Mrs Lambchop's hand. 'We should be very proud of our son, Harriet.'

Mrs Lambchop thought for a moment. 'Stanley,' she said at last. 'Will you be very, very, careful not to let that enormous building fall on you?'

'Okay. Sure,' Stanley said.

Mrs Lambchop turned to Mr and Mrs Weeks. 'We will allow Stanley to help,' she said. 'He will do his best for Emma.'

'Fine boy we got here! Brave as a lion!' shouted Chief Johnson. 'Now listen up, folks! Mrs Lambchop, you help me get things ready! Then Stanley can go right in after Emma! Got that? Everybody meet us at the Merker Building, thirty minutes from now!'

Chapter Seven

Where Are You, Emma?

In the late afternoon sunlight, at the remains of the old Merker Building, the Lambchops and the Weekses watched Chief Johnson prepare Stanley for his rescue attempt. Flash Tobin, the *Daily Sentinel* photographer, was there too, taking pictures.

Mrs Lambchop had supplied two slices of bread and cheese, each wrapped in plastic, and her grandfather's flat silver cigarette case filled with fizzy grape drink. Chief Johnson taped the bread and cheese packets to Stanley's arms and legs, the cigarette case to his chest, and gave him a small, flat torch.

Then he led Stanley up to a tall crack in the wreckage. 'Emma!' he shouted. 'Fella's coming to help you! When he calls your name, you holler back "Here!" so he knows which way to go. Got that?'

Emma's voice came faintly. 'Yeah, yeah! Hurry up! I'm starving!'

Chief Johnson shook Stanley's hand. 'Get goin', son!'

The evening sunlight glowed warmly on the red bricks of the fallen building as

Stanley stepped close to the crack. Mrs Lambchop waved to him, and Stanley waved back. How handsome he is, she thought. How brave, how tall, how flat!

Stanley took two steps forward and disappeared sideways through the crack. A moment later they heard his shout. 'Hey! It's really dark in here!'

'Hay is for horses, Stanley!' Mrs Lambchop called back. 'Oh, never mind! Good luck, dear!'

This was a dark greater than any he had ever known. Stanley could almost feel the blackness on his skin. He clicked his torch and edged forward without difficulty, but then the crack narrowed, slowing him. The bread slice on his left leg had scraped something, loosening the tape that held it. Pressing the tape back into place, he wiggled forward until he came to what seemed a dead end, but a little swing of the torch showed cracks branching right and left.

'Emma?' he called.

'Here!'

Her voice came from the right, so he moved along that branch. 'Emma?'

'Yeah, yeah! What?'

'When I say your name, you're supposed to say "Here!"'

'I already did that!'

He followed another crack to the left. 'Emma?'

There was no answer. Stanley managed a few more feet and then, quite suddenly, the crack widened. He called again. 'Emma?'

'Bananas!'

'Keep talking,' he shouted. 'I need to hear you!'

'Bananas! Here! Blah, blah! Whatever! Hey, I can see your light!'

And there she was. The crack had widened to become a small cave, at the back of which sat Emma. Her jeans and shirt were smudged with dirt, but it was most surely Emma, squinting against the brightness of his light.

'You!' she exclaimed. 'From school! The flattie!'

Don't lose your temper, Stanley told himself. 'I was the only one they thought could get in here. How are you doing, Emma?'

Emma rolled her eyes. 'Oh, just great!

A whole building falls on me, and they send in a flattie! And now I'm starving to death!'

Stanley untaped the slices of bread and cheese, and handed them over.

'Cheese, huh?' Emma put her sandwich together and took a bite. 'I hate cheese. Got anything to drink, flattie?'

'Please don't call me flattie. Here.' He held out the silver cigarette case.

Emma rolled her eyes again. 'I'm not allowed to smoke.'

'It's fizzy drink.'

She opened the cigarette case and sipped. 'Blaahh! I hate grape!'

Chief Johnson's voice rose from a hole in the wall behind her. 'Stanley? You there yet?'

Emma jerked a thumb at the hole. 'It's for you, flattie.'

'I'm here, Chief!' Stanley called. 'Emma's okay.'

He heard cheering, and then the Chief's voice came again. 'See a way out, Stan?'

'I haven't had a chance to look around yet. Emma's eating.'

'We'll wait. Over and out, Stan!'

'You too!' Stanley called.

He waited until Emma had finished her sandwich. 'Emma, how did you get into this mess? What made you come in here?'

'I just came over to look,' Emma said. 'And they had all these signs! "Danger! Keep out!" All over the place, even behind in the parking lot. "Keep out! Danger!

Danger!" I really hate that, you know? So there was this door, and it was open, so I went in.' She finished the fizzy grape drink. 'Okay, let's go.'

'Not the way I came in,' Stanley said. 'I could just barely squeeze through. And we have to be careful, because –'

'I know!' Emma interrupted. 'Chief whatshisname kept telling me: "Don't move around! The whole rest of the building might crash down!" So am I supposed to live down here forever?'

'This door you came through,' Stanley said. 'How far did you come to find this sort of cave we're in?'

'Who said anything about far? I just got inside, and there were these crashing noises, and the whole building was shaking, and I fell down right here! The crashing went on forever! I thought I was going to die!'

'Calm down.' An idea came into Stanley's head. 'Just where was this door? Do you remember?'

'Over there somewhere.' Emma pointed into the darkness of a corner behind her.

Stanley swung his light, but saw only what seemed to be a solid wall of splintered boards, rock, and brick.

Emma pointed a bit left, then right. 'Maybe there . . . I don't know! Was I supposed to take pictures or something? What difference does it make?'

'We might be just a little bit inside that

door,' Stanley said. 'And what we want is
to be just outside of it.'

Moving closer to the corner, he saw that
a jagged piece of wood protruded at waist
level. It came out easily when he tugged,
followed by loose dirt.

Emma stood beside him. 'Why are you

making this mess?'

He poked in the hole with the stick. 'Maybe I'll find —'

Dirt cascaded from the wall, covering his shoes. He saw light now, not just the little circle from his torch, but daylight! Unmistakably daylight!

'Oooohhhh!' said Emma.

Stanley made the hole still larger, and they saw that a door lay on its side across the bottom of the hole, wreckage limiting the opening on both sides. But it was big enough! They would be able to wiggle through! He ran back to the wall from which Chief Johnson's voice had come.

'We're on our way out!' he shouted. 'We'll be at the back, in the courtyard!'

'Got it!' came the Chief's voice. 'Great work!'

Stanley turned to Emma. 'Let's go!'

'I'll get all dirty, silly,' Emma said. 'Maybe we could just –'

'Come ON!'

'Don't yell!' Emma said, but she crawled quickly through the hole with Stanley right behind her.

Hero!

There was much rejoicing in the courtyard. Mrs Lambchop kissed Stanley and Arthur. Mrs Weeks kissed Emma, and then everyone else, even Flash Tobin, who had arrived to take pictures. Mr Lambchop shook hands with Mr Weeks and Chief Johnson, who announced several times that Stanley was a great hero.

Flash Tobin took a group picture of all

the Lambchops. 'Need one more,' he said. 'Emma, just you and Stanley. Your hero, right? Saved your life!'

'I could have got out by myself,' Emma said. 'I just didn't know exactly where the door was.' But she went to stand by Stanley.

'Smile!' Flash Tobin took the picture. 'Yes, that's good!' He gave Stanley a cheerful slap on the back, just as Emma's elbow jabbed hard into Stanley's ribs.

'Owww!' Stanley yelled.

Emma grinned. 'That's for you, Mr Hero!'

'Are you crazy? What —' Stanley stopped. Everybody was staring at him. He felt peculiar, as if — Yes! He was getting round again!

'Wow!' Emma said. 'How do you do that?'

'Hooray for you, dear!' shouted Mrs Lambchop, and more cries rose from the others in the courtyard. 'Do you see what I see? . . . He's blowing up! . . . Are we crazy or what?'

Flash Tobin aimed his camera again. 'Hold it, kid!'

But he was too late. Before him now stood a smiling Stanley Lambchop, shaped like a regular boy!

Mr Lambchop ran to hug him, and everyone else applauded.

'Thirty years with the Fire Department, and I never saw anything like that!' said Chief Johnson. 'Wouldn't have missed it!'

'I'm really glad,' Stanley said. 'But what made it happen?'

'What Doctor Dan said!' shouted Arthur. 'Remember? The Osteo–posteo–whatever!'

'The OBP! The Osteal Balance Point.' Mr Lambchop smiled. 'Yes! The slap on the back from Flash Tobin, and the poke from Emma! That did it!'

A board fell from the tilting roof of the Merker Building, landing in a corner of the courtyard.

'Let's go, folks,' said Chief Johnson. 'We're not safe here!'

Everyone went home.

Fame!

At bedtime the next evening, the Lambchops read again the *Daily Sentinel* they had enjoyed so much at breakfast that morning.

The front page headline read: RUDE GIRL SAVED! FLAT RESCUER REGAINS SHAPE! Beneath that were two Flash Tobin photographs, the Lambchop family picture, and the

RUDE GIRL SAVED
FLAT RESCUER
REGAINS SHAPE!

one of Stanley and Emma taken just before she poked him in the ribs. Arthur was particularly pleased with the family picture.

'Finally!' he said. 'Not just Stanley! People could have been wondering if he had a brother, you know? Can I have this one?'

'You may,' said Mrs Lambchop. 'I want the one of Stanley with Emma, for my kitchen wall.'

'I don't care about pictures,' Stanley said. 'I just hope I never go back to being flat.'

Mrs Lambchop patted his hand. 'I told Dr Dan of your recovery, dear. He thinks it most unlikely the flatness will occur again.'

'Yay!' said Stanley.

Arthur cut the family picture out of the paper, and used a red pencil to draw an

arrow, pointing up at him, in the white space at the bottom. Under the arrow, he wrote, *Hero's Brother*! Then he taped the picture to the wall above his bed.

Soon all the Lambchops were asleep.

Whoever heard of a flat ninja?

Stanley is a huge fan of the ninja movie star Oda Nobu. So he decides to send something even better than fan mail – himself!

Soon enough, Flat Stanley is in Japan with Oda Nobu. But trouble is not far behind. Lucky that they have their ninja moves!

Stanley is in the Wild West!

The whole Lambchop family is off to see Mount Rushmore. But when Flat Stanley and his brother meet a cowgirl named Calamity Jasper, they get into a really tight spot.

Can Stanley help them get out again?

Stanley is as flat as a pancake and can fit into places that no one else can . . .

So when he receives a letter from an archaeologist asking for his help, he posts himself by airmail to Egypt!

Can Stanley find the ancient treasure hidden in the pyramid? He'll have to beat the tomb raiders first!

The Australian Boomerang Bonanza
written by J. Greenhut
created by Jeff Brown

Stanley and his brother Arthur have just won a trip to Australia! They fly Down Under on a private jet and go diving in the Great Barrier Reef.

But when Arthur launches him into the air for a game of boomerang, Stanley is accidentally sent spinning off into the heart of the Australian outback!